Go Wild

Look out for other books
by Julian Clary & David Roberts:

The Bolds

The Bolds to the Rescue

The Bolds on Holiday

The Bolds in Trouble

The Bolds' Great Adventure
(a World Book Day book)

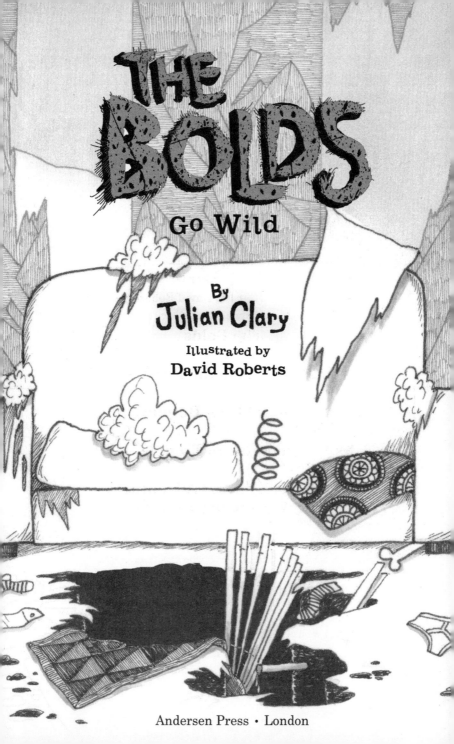

THE BOLDS

Go Wild

By
Julian Clary

Illustrated by
David Roberts

Andersen Press · London

First published in 2019 by
Andersen Press Limited
20 Vauxhall Bridge Road
London SW1V 2SA
www.andersenpress.co.uk

2 4 6 8 10 9 7 5 3 1

British Library Cataloguing in Publication Data available.

ISBN 978 1 78344 804 3

This book is printed on FSC accredited paper from responsible sources.
Printed and bound in Great Britain by Clays Ltd, Elcograf S.p.A.

For Milo

Chapter

Some people think that everything happens for a reason. This makes perfect sense to me. Although sometimes it can take a while for the reason to become clear. You just have to be patient, that's all.

Why did I lose a shoe on the way to school? It was certainly very annoying; my foot got wet and my mother was cross with me. BUT . . . losing the shoe meant I was late for class and so I missed a maths exam. Result! It happened for a reason.

And I once told my best friend that I still slept with a teddy called Mr Pilchard. My friend told the whole class and they all laughed at me. But then I realised the reason for all this upset: it was time to dump my best friend and get myself one who *could* be trusted. So I did.

Now what about the things that happen to the Bolds?

Perhaps you are new to stories about them. I hope not, because that would mean you've been missing out on lots of fun. The Bolds, you see, are a family that strange things happen to – some things good, some not so good – but always for a reason. The good things are wonderful and the not-so-good always make the stories about them very interesting – though I say so myself.

Our story this time begins on a rainy day. Most people on days like that want to stay indoors and avoid getting wet. This isn't the case with the Bolds, though. Dear me, no. They love the rain. Rain means puddles and mud, both of which they are very keen on. Stamping in puddles and making a mess, getting mud in their fur, down their trousers or anywhere else you can think of, is their idea of fun. This is probably because the Bolds family, as you may already know, aren't actually people.

No. They're hyenas. Hyenas living disguised as human beings in a lovely little house in Teddington. In order to keep this unusual fact a secret, they are careful not to do anything too hyena-ish in public: no running around on all fours, no chasing things and eating them, no rubbing their bottoms on bushes.

But laughing wildly and messing about in the rain and mud are hyena traits they can get away with. And they do. People might think them a little odd, but those same people never jump to the conclusion that the family running around and laughing in the rain are hyenas. And for the Bolds it is a little taste of their old life. It satisfies their hyena instincts, so carefully covered up most of the time.

So on this particular day in early April, during a heavy shower, the Bold family (Mr and Mrs Bold, and their twins, Bobby and

Betty) spent a glorious couple of hours in a rather wet Bushy Park. They took with them their fellow hyena Uncle Tony, and Miranda the marmoset monkey, as well as their next-door neighbour Mr McNumpty (who is a grizzly bear, not a hyena, but rather partial to a frolic in the mud nevertheless).

To begin with they just hopped over puddles, laughing and shrieking. But then Bobby landed in a large one (perhaps by mistake, perhaps not) and splashed water all over Betty's skirt.

'Right! Game on!' said a laughing Betty, before jumping in the air and landing with a splat! right in the middle of an even larger, ominously dark puddle. It turned out this puddle was much deeper than expected. Betty suddenly found herself knee-deep in filthy muddy water. And not only was Bobby drenched from head to foot in thick gravy-like mud, but Mrs Bold was too, as she happened to have been walking just behind Bobby.

Now I don't know about *your* family, but in mine Betty and Bobby would be in big trouble by now. However things are a little different with the Bolds.

'Eek!' said Betty, covering her mouth with her paws in surprise.

'You've had it now, Sis!' laughed Bobby,

jumping in beside his sister, creating a new wave that curled right up and engulfed a squealing Betty's neck.

Mrs Bold, meanwhile, simply inhaled the earthy scent and her nostrils twitched with delight. She gave Mr Bold a sly glance. 'Mmmm!' she said. 'This *so* reminds me of life in Africa during the rainy season. Have a sniff, Fred!' She scooped up a handful of mud and rubbed it over Mr Bold's face.

'Ahhh!' said her husband. 'I know what you mean, Amelia.'

What did one raindrop say to the other?

My plop is bigger than your plop!

Now, in case you are unaware, Mr Bold loves jokes. Many dads do. But unlike lots of dads' jokes, Mr Bold's are actually funny and he even has a job writing them for Christmas crackers. A pretty cool job, don't you think?

When his wife heard his latest joke she threw her head back with laughter, and her hat (a home-made bonnet made from a round cake tin decorated with several empty tomato soup tins and some cleverly folded napkins) fell into the mud. But before she could pick it up, Uncle Tony (who was bent over on account of his arthritis) grabbed hold of the tin, scooped up some dirty water and, with a hyena howl of mischievous laughter, flung it over his best friend Mr McNumpty.

Nigel McNumpty wasted no time before retaliating: he reached into the depths of the deep puddle, smothering his designer-suit sleeves with muck in the process, and flung a heavy lump of smelly mud at his friend. The mud ball hit Uncle Tony a glancing blow on the shoulder but somehow landed on Mr Bold's face where it slid slowly down to his chest, leaving a gleaming brown trail behind.

Momentarily shocked, Mr Bold then let out a distinctly animal-like cackle.

Ha ha ha! What does a cloud wear under its raincoat?

Thunderwear!

Mrs Bold was so busy laughing at her husband's joke that she didn't notice Uncle Tony now creeping up behind her with Miranda perched on his shoulder, and the cake tin, full of water, in her little monkey paws. When they were directly behind her, Miranda tipped the tin all over Mrs Bold, and Uncle Tony stood there shaking with laughter.

'Bullseye! Me wetty Missy Boldy!' laughed Miranda.

Well, it was sheer mayhem after that, I can tell you. Luckily no one was out in the park that day, so no humans were there to see the extraordinary sight of a family rolling about in cold muddy puddles, hooting with delight.

After an hour or more of this pandemonium – like a snowball fight with mud that got way out of control – the Bolds pulled themselves together again.

'We'd better stop,' said Mrs Bold breathlessly. 'Before we are seen. Please, Bobby, don't do that in the ferns – it's not at all human-like.'

Exhausted, but exhilarated and very, very happy (hyena happy), they made their way home to 41 Fairfield Road.

'Right,' said Mr Bold with a sigh when they were safely inside the house. 'We'd better all get changed into some clean, dry clothes.'

There was a bit of a queue for the bathroom, but a couple of hours later everyone was clean and dry and sitting in the lounge enjoying hot buttered crumpets, slices of fruit cake and milky tea. The twins' best friend Minnie, the only human who knew the Bolds' secret, had come round. But being a human she wasn't so keen on wet weather and couldn't understand why her friends had got themselves so muddy like that.

'What goes up when rain comes down?' Mr Bold asked her.

'I know the answer to that,' said Minnie. 'An umbrella!'

'Yes!' Mr Bold said. 'Although we don't own one in this house. Can't think of anything more silly than avoiding the rain. In the Serengeti it only ever rains in the rainy season. So when it does, we animals get very excited. We all get as wet as possible. I remember my mother teaching me and my brothers and sisters how to roll around in the mud. It's good for our skin and keeps mosquitos away.' Mr Bold stared into the distance. 'Ah, yes,' he sighed. 'Happy days.'

But his thoughts of home were suddenly interrupted by an urgent tapping sound.

'What's that?' asked Bobby.

'It's coming from the window!' declared Mrs Bold, pulling back the net curtains to get a closer look. There, on the other side of the window, sat a fairly large, sleek grey bird, his beady eyes staring in through the glass. He gave three quick, impatient taps with his small beak and then sat there expectantly.

'He wants to come in out of the rain,' said Mrs Bold. 'All right, Mr Bird! One moment.'

And she opened the window to let him in.

Chapter

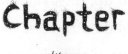

The second the window was open, the bird flew in and perched on top of the television, looking round the room.

'Hello there,' said Uncle Tony, who was just finishing a slice of fruit cake. 'Can I interest you in these crumbs?' He held out his plate in the direction of the bird, who looked at them hungrily.

'Thank you,' he said. 'That is most kind. Could someone bring them over here? I've had rather a long flight and my wings are all flapped out.'

Betty jumped up, took the plate from Uncle Tony and rested it on the television next to the bird – who immediately began to eat all the golden crumbs.

'Delicious!' he said with his beak full.

While he ate, the Bolds were able to admire his lovely plumage. It was dark grey on his back, but much lighter over his chest, with stripes of darker feathers from chin to legs. His head was a soft, pale dove-grey and he had a short, yellowish beak that curved downwards, and startled-looking eyes of even brighter yellow with a black centre. Very quickly the crumbs had all gone and the bird looked around expectantly.

'Would you like some more?' asked Mrs Bold.

'Well, I don't suppose you have any caterpillars? Or a grasshopper, do you?'

'Er, I saw some caterpillars on the cabbages in your vegetable patch this morning, Fred,' said Mr McNumpty.

'I'll go and get you some,' offered Betty. She took the plate and went out to the garden.

While she was gone, Mr Bold filled in the silence with some jokes.

Where does a caterpillar buy his clothes?

A cater-logue!

It wasn't one of his best jokes, but the hungry bird seemed to appreciate it. The bird's laugh was most unusual, a sort of 'coo, coo, coo!' sound.

Encouraged by his reaction, Mr Bold tried another joke.

What's a caterpillar's favourite weapon?

A cater-pault!

The bird nodded appreciatively and again let out his gentle 'coo-coo' laugh.

What is the definition of a caterpillar?

A worm in a fur coat!

'Oh, that one is very good,' complimented the bird. 'Your jokes are quite a tonic after my long journey.'

'Have you come far?'

'Three thousand, five hundred and eighty-three miles,' the bird answered nonchalantly, giving his chest feathers a gentle peck with his beak.

'Wowsers!' said Bobby, impressed. 'No wonder you're so hungry. Did you do it all in one go?'

'Er, no,' said the bird. 'I had a comfort break in Morocco and then I ate so much pasta in Italy I couldn't take off for a week.'

Just then Betty arrived back from the garden with seven or eight green wriggling

20

caterpillars on a plate. Despite being so tired, the bird flapped his wings with delight.

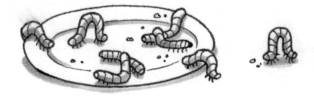

'Ah, thank you! The crumbs were a very nice starter, but this is my main course!' He deftly picked up the first caterpillar with his beak, tilted his head back slightly, and it was gone. 'Heaven!' he sighed. 'I haven't had one of these tasty fellas since I left England six months ago. My name is Hector, by the way.'

There was an awful lot the Bolds wanted to know. Where had Hector been? Why had he flown back? And why had he tapped on their window?

But they all sat in polite silence while

Hector enjoyed his dinner, which, it has to be said, didn't take long. When the last juicy caterpillar disappeared into his yellow beak he sighed contentedly again. 'Thank you, thank you!' he said. 'You are all very kind. Now would you mind terribly, Fred, if I had a little sleep?'

Fred looked surprised. 'Er, no, of course not. But how do you know my name?'

Hector didn't answer. 'I could perch on the curtain rail, if that's all right with you?' he suggested, yawning and blinking with evident tiredness. He didn't wait for a reply and flew the short distance to the window, settling himself in the corner. 'Perhaps you'd better put some newspaper down on the floor below me?' he added. 'I sometimes do my business in my sleep. Embarrassing really, but that's our cuckoo way.'

'You're a cuckoo?' asked Bobby, looking up at the bird, who ruffled his feathers.

Hector's head drooped as he gave another yawn and his eyes began to close. 'I am, yes. I'll tell you everything when I wake up. I'm really sorry, but I am so, so tired now. I've come to tell Fred something very important. But it will have to wait . . . until . . . morn . . . ing.' Hector's eyes closed altogether and within seconds there was a gentle 'COO-COO-ZZZ' noise.

'But . . . !' began Fred.

'Not now,' whispered Mrs Bold. 'He's snoring. No wonder, after that long journey. Let the poor bird have some rest. Let's leave him in peace.' She turned out the lights and signalled for everyone to leave the room. They all crept out in silence.

I don't know about you, but I'm not very good at being patient. If someone told me they had something 'very important' to tell me and then fell asleep, my imagination would be working overtime. Is it good news or bad news? Will it make me happy or cross or sad? I'd have to wake them up somehow.

Well, poor Mr Bold felt exactly the same. He poked his head round the lounge door several times that evening but Hector was always fast asleep. He tried to pass the time by telling jokes, of course. Telling jokes was always what Fred did in any situation. He found it relaxing.

What do you get if you cross a clock with a chicken?

A cluck!

What did the robber
say to the clock?

"Hands up!"

What did the watch
say to the clock?

"Hour you
doing?"

But even so, it was a very long evening for
Fred as he waited and waited.

Eventually Minnie went home, and the
twins had their cocoa and their bedtime story.

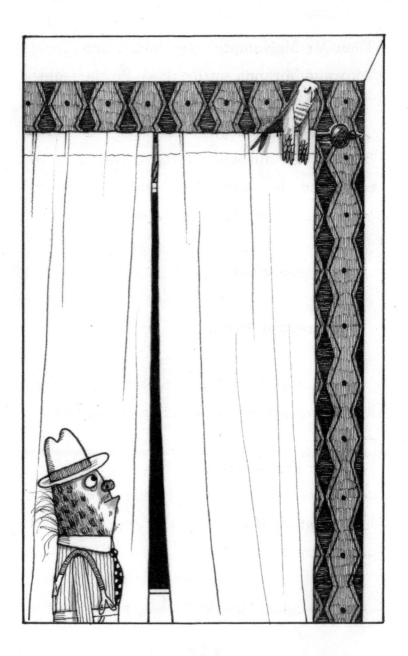

Then Mr McNumpty went home, and Uncle Tony and Miranda settled down for the night.

'It's nearly half past ten, Fred,' said Mrs Bold to her husband. 'I think Hector is so exhausted he will sleep until tomorrow morning. We will just have to wait.'

'Wait?' said Fred.

'Yes,' replied Amelia.

'But I can't!' said her husband. He tried loudly whispering 'Hector!' but it didn't work.

Hector kept on sleeping.

'How about if I accidentally drop a tin tray outside the lounge door?'

'No,' laughed Mrs Bold. 'I won't hear of it.'

'Or I could have a coughing fit?'

'You haven't got a cough!'

'But I'm desperate to know Hector's news . . . what can it be?'

'You'll find out in the morning, dear. Try and think about something else.'

Chapter

It was a **difficult** night for Mr Bold. He couldn't get to sleep for hours, wondering about Hector's news. Then he was awake before dawn, washed and dressed and listening outside the lounge door to see if their visitor had woken up. He hadn't. So Fred collected some more caterpillars from the vegetable patch ready for Hector's breakfast. In fact, he tried one himself and rather **enjoyed** it. So he tried **another**. Then **another**, until in the end he had to make a second trip to the garden to replenish the saucer.

Eventually everyone else got up and had

breakfast and they all gathered in the lounge, facing the still-sleeping cuckoo. The twins began to giggle. Mr Bold cleared his throat rather loudly. Then Uncle Tony had one of his wheezing fits and that did the trick. Hector slowly opened one eye, then the other. He yawned and looked around him as if he couldn't quite remember where he was.

'Er, good morning, Hector,' said Mr Bold brightly. 'I hope you slept well?'

'Yes, thank you, I did,' replied Hector sleepily.

'Breakfast?' offered Mrs Bold, holding

up the saucer with about a dozen wriggling caterpillars on it. Hector immediately flew down from the curtain rail to the coffee table and set about eating them. As soon as the last one was finished, Mr Bold could contain himself no longer.

'You said you had come to tell me something important?'

Hector wiped his beak on his chest and nodded. 'Yes. You are Fred Bold? And this is Number 41 Fairfield Road, Teddington, Middlesex, in England?'

'Yes, yes, yes,' said Mr Bold. 'I am and it is. What is the news?'

'Do you have any proof of identity? Passport? Utility bills? Photo ID?'

Mr Bold stood up and looked in the mirror that hung above the fireplace. 'Yes, that's definitely me,' he said confidently.

'Excellent. Then I will begin,' said Hector. 'Listen carefully.'

Everyone's attention was focused on the grey bird sitting on the coffee table.

'A little background information is important, I feel,' began Hector, before clearing his throat.

'My name is Hector and I am a cuckoo. Cuckoos are medium-sized, sleek birds, just like me, with soft feathers and long tails to help us steer. We enjoy a cosmopolitan distribution, mostly in tropical places, it's fair to say, as we prefer to live in trees. We eat insects, insect larvae and various other bits and bobs, as well as fruit. Some cuckoos are known as "brood parasites", which means they sneakily lay their eggs in other birds' nests and let them have the bother of raising the hatchlings, but some also raise their own young. It just depends what mood we are in.'

Bobby and Betty let out a simultaneous sigh. This was not as interesting as they had thought it was going to be.

Mrs Bold gave them a stern look. 'Shhh!' she whispered. 'This is very educational.'

'Cuckoos have always played an interesting role in human culture,' continued Hector. 'Notably in Greek mythology, where you may or may not know they are considered sacred to the goddess Hera. In Japan, cuckoos symbolise unrequited love, while here in Europe, our call heralds the beginning of spring to many. Isn't that interesting?'

Mr Bold couldn't contain his impatience. 'Yes, Hector, yes. But what is the news you have for me?'

'I'm getting to that,' said Hector. 'I am of the migratory variety of cuckoo. I spend April to October here in England and then I fly many miles south to avoid your winter months.'

'Where do you go?' asked Mr McNumpty.

'Africa,' replied Hector.

Suddenly everyone's ears pricked up.

'Africa?' said Mr Bold, a slight tremble in his voice. 'But that is where we come from.'

'I know,' said Hector simply. 'And it is from Africa that I bring your news.'

Fred and Amelia looked at each other, eyes wide with amazement.

'Please continue,' said Fred. 'What is the

important news you have for me?'

Hector cleared his throat again. 'Do you think I might have some water? I'm a little dry, and after such a long time getting here I'm not used to all this talking.'

You could have fooled me, thought Mr Bold, but he said nothing. Bobby jumped up and went to the kitchen, returning with a saucer of water for the cuckoo.

'Thank you so much,' said Hector, before taking several long sips. Then he began talking again.

'Africa is the second largest continent in the world, with the second largest population. It covers eleven point seven million square miles in fact, making up twenty per cent of all the land on planet Earth. Africa is surrounded by bodies of water, including the *Mediterranean Sea* to the north, the *Suez Canal* and the *Red Sea* along the *Sinai Peninsula* to the north-east, the *Atlantic Ocean* to the west and the *Indian Ocean* to the south-east.'

Hector was then interrupted by the sound of snoring.

'*Uncle Tony*,' said Mr McNumpty, giving his friend a nudge. 'Wake up!'

'Oh, er, sorry,' said Uncle Tony. 'Have we got to the important news yet?'

'Afraid not,' said Mr Bold.

'May I continue?' asked Hector.

'Oh, yes please,' said Mrs Bold. 'You mentioned some news?'

'Just getting to that,' said Hector. 'Now, where was I? Ah, yes. The continent is mostly situated in the *northern hemisphere,* but there are still a number of African countries in the *southern hemisphere.*'

The twins began to giggle. 'This is worse than being at school!' said Betty.

'Yes, definitely,' replied Bobby. 'At least we get a packed lunch at school.'

Mrs Bold glared at them, although secretly she quite agreed.

Hector droned on: 'There are many native animals in Africa. Too many to list just now—'

'Quite,' jumped in Mr Bold. 'We don't want to be here all day!'

'Perhaps some of the best-known are the lion, elephant, giraffe, leopard, rhino, cheetah, buffalo, crocodile, hippopotamus and zebra,' continued Hector. 'I have seen all of these animals in my time, I'm pleased to say.'

'What about hyenas?' asked Fred, a little indignantly.

'Yes, hyenas too,' confirmed Hector.

'Now we're getting somewhere,' muttered Mr McNumpty.

Hector cleared his throat again. 'Hyenas are very interesting animals. A bit like a mix-up of a cat and a dog. Hyenas catch their prey using their jaws, then eat very quickly, or sometimes store their food somewhere secret. They have calloused feet with large, non-retractable, blunt claws, handy for running and turning.'

The twins both looked at their paws during this speech. 'See?' said Bobby to his sister. 'I knew there was a reason we had such big hands!'

'Hyenas are, generally speaking, nocturnal animals,' continued Hector. 'But sometimes they venture out from their lairs first thing in the morning.'

'Er, we don't do that any more,' pointed out Mrs Bold. 'The neighbours were beginning to talk.'

'Over time hyenas evolved into two distinct types: the almost extinct, lightly built, dog-like hyenas and the more familiar robust, bone-crushing hyenas.'

'That's us!' said Betty, punching the air. 'We are the bone-crushing Bolds!'

'Hyenas, like cuckoos, often appear in the folklore of human cultures. For example—'

But Mr Bold could take no more. 'Hector, I hate to interrupt you again. But we *are* hyenas. You don't need to tell us all this. We know it already.'

'But I'm just getting into my stride,' said Hector, sounding a little hurt.

Surprisingly it was Miranda – usually shy and retiring – who put a stop to Hector's monologue once and for all. She suddenly leaped out from inside Uncle Tony's T-shirt and landed next to the cuckoo on the coffee table. She placed a gentle hand on Hector's back and spoke quietly to him.

'You talky too much! We getty bored listen to you. On and on you go. Why you no tell us newsy?'

'Oh, but I thought a little background information might be helpful,' explained Hector.

'No. You boring,' said Miranda bluntly.

'I do apologise.' Hector ruffled his feathers. 'When I'm on these long flights I pass the time by reciting as many facts as I can remember from the encyclopaedia.'

'Why you no watch filmy?' asked Miranda.

'I'm the one doing the flying,' said Hector. 'I'm not on an aeroplane. There's no in-flight service!'

'Ohhhhh!' said Miranda. 'Me understandy now. No wonder you so boring.'

'I'll do as you ask,' said Hector, pursing his beak. 'I'll tell you the important news you are all waiting for.'

Chapter

Everyone held their breath and leaned forward to hear what Hector had to say.

'So,' said Hector. 'As I have explained, I am a cuckoo. I have just flown in from Africa where I spent the last five months in an area known as the Serengeti.'

Mr and Mrs Bold let out a gasp. 'That's where we come from!' said Mrs Bold.

'Our home!' declared Mr Bold.

Hector nodded sagely. 'Yes. I know. I had

just taken a refreshing bath on the edge of a lake on the plains there one morning. Some zebras were nearby and I could tell they were a little on edge, nervous about something.'

'Lions, I expect!' said Bobby.

'Or a hungry cheetah!' speculated Betty.

'Well, no, as it happens it was neither of those creatures. I hopped up onto the back of a zebra to see what was going on and I saw a family of hyenas lurking in the tall grass. A family of about ten or so, moving in fast. I told the zebra that she and her friends were in danger. She thanked me, and the whole herd of zebra stopped drinking from the lake immediately and galloped away as fast as they could.'

'Humph!' said Mr Bold. 'How annoying for the hyenas!'

'Indeed,' agreed Hector. 'There was a big cloud of dust and I flew up into the branches of an acacia tree, and I heard what those hyenas had to say. Very colourful language!' Hector rolled his eyes at the memory. 'I couldn't possibly repeat it.'

Mr Bold chuckled. 'Ha ha! Never get in the way of a hyena and his dinner!'

'I felt a little sorry for them, though,' continued Hector. 'They had young, growing pups with them who looked particularly peckish. I hopped down a few branches in the tree to get closer to the hyenas. Still out of reach, mind, but within earshot. "So sorry," I said. "The zebras are my friends, so I felt I had to warn them that you were closing in."

'"We've just wasted the last hour creeping through the long grass!" said a very angry female hyena. She was bigger than the others, and clearly in charge. "My pups haven't eaten all day! Why did you have to interfere? I've a good mind to climb up there and eat *you*. Although from what I can see there isn't a lot of meat on you. You'd just be a snack."'

'True,' said Mr Bold. It was wonderful to hear stories of wild hyenas – especially as these ones were from the very part of Africa that he and Mrs Bold once called home.

'So what did you do next?' asked Mrs Bold. 'Did you fly away?'

'No,' replied Hector. 'The four little hyena pups looked so disappointed and so hungry, I had an idea to help the hyenas.'

'Bravo!' said Uncle Tony, who was now wide awake.

'I told the female hyena about something I had observed earlier: a leopard had killed an antelope just half a mile or so away. She hadn't eaten it but had hidden it under some brush. If they followed me I would show the hyenas where a meal was waiting for them.'

Mrs Bold started to dribble at the distant memory of a nice, tasty antelope, so she quickly produced a handkerchief from her handbag and wiped her chin. 'What a kind thing to do,' she said.

'There are over ninety different species of antelope, most of which are native to Africa,' Hector began to explain, but Miranda quickly held up her paw.

'No starty explain antelopes please!' she said sternly.

'Just carry on with what happened with the hyenas,' said Betty encouragingly.

'Very well,' said Hector, pausing to take several long sips of water. 'I flew in the direction of the antelope, and the hyenas followed me. They squealed and whooped with delight when we got there, then they all tucked in. The leopard came to retrieve her kill eventually, but not before all the hyena family had had plenty to eat.'

'Ah,' said Mr Bold dreamily. 'Life in the wild, eh? This takes me back. Hunting and scavenging for food rather than queuing up in the supermarket.'

'After their feed, the hyenas found a nice shady spot under a tree where they settled down for an afternoon sleep. The mother hyena was so grateful for my assistance she suggested I join them. "How about you hop onto my back and help yourself to the fleas that live in my fur?" she said. Well, I love fleas – they are delicious. But I was cautious. Hyenas are clever and – how shall I put it? – sometimes a little devious. Getting up close with a hyena might be risky.'

The Bolds looked more than a little offended at the suggestion.

'You mean, you thought her offer might be a trick?' asked Mr McNumpty, his eyes narrowing.

'Yes,' confessed Hector. 'If I was sitting on the

hyena's back, what was to stop her reaching round and swallowing me in one gulp?'

'But you had been so kind and helpful,' argued Bobby. 'Surely she wouldn't hurt you after that?'

'Well, I looked into her deep, amber eyes and saw that she was being truthful. It wasn't a trick. I jumped onto her back and began to gobble up the fleas as she snoozed. After a while I was quite full and nodded off myself, right there on her back!'

'How sweet!' declared Betty.

'What a lovely story,' said Uncle Tony. 'Thank you very much for sharing it.'

'But I haven't got to the best bit yet,' exclaimed Hector.

'There's more?' asked Tony.

'There is. The hyenas and I began to spend our days together. I would fly high for a look around and tell them where there was something to eat. Then I would help myself to the fleas and bugs, ticks and parasites, that lived on their backs.'

'You scratch their back and they scratch yours!' said Mr McNumpty, rather pleased with his summing up of the situation.

'Quite so,' agreed Hector. 'An unusual but mutually beneficial inter-species arrangement.'

Miranda shot Hector a warning glance.

'Over the days and weeks we enjoyed nice chats together. The weather, our lives, our hopes for the future. We grew to like each other. To trust each other, even. I also played hide-and-seek with the pups, although they were a little boisterous, and I had to be ready to fly out of their reach if the game got too rough.'

Bobby and Betty looked at each other and giggled.

'Then one day I asked the mother hyena if these were her first pups. She said she had had several litters, and pointed out her older children amongst the other hyenas sleeping nearby. Then to my surprise her eyes filled with tears. She had had one pup, she said, who was cleverer, funnier and braver than all the others.

'"Where is that pup now?" I asked. The hyena stared into the distance. "He has gone, far, far away." "To the other side of the Serengeti?"

I asked. "No. Further than that," she said, through her tears. "Much further. I miss him so much. My Spot. He went to start a new life in England."'

Mr Bold let out a cry and stood up, slapping a paw against his forehead in shock.

'Oh, my my!' he cried. 'That's me! I am Spot! Well, I mean I used to be called Spot when I was a wild hyena in Africa. I changed my name to Fred Bold when I left for England.'

Mrs Bold stood up too, and put her arm round her husband.

'Oh, Spot!' she said. 'Hector was with your mother!'

'Yes,' confirmed Hector.

Mr Bold shook his head in astonishment. 'I can hardly believe it!' he said. 'I thought, as you told the story, that she sounded like my dear old mother. And I have new brothers and sisters too!'

'You do,' nodded Hector. 'All very well and happy.'

'Well, I'll be blowed,' said Mr McNumpty.

'I miss my mother and my home so much. It is wonderful to hear your news,' said Mr Bold, wiping his eyes. 'But can it really be true? Did the hyena say what her name was?'

'Yes. Her name was Imamu,' said Hector softly.

Fred was overcome with another flood of tears. 'Yes, yes, that is my mother's name. Imamu. My dear mother!'

'Grandma!' said the twins. 'Our granny Imamu!' They jumped up too and all the Bolds hugged each other.

'I have one more bit of news for you,' said Hector after a few minutes, when everyone had settled down again.

'Yes?' asked Fred. 'What more news can there be?'

'A few days before I began my migration back here to England, Imamu went away for a few hours to speak to someone. She returned

looking very happy and determined. "I'd like you to take a message to my Spot in England," she said. She made me promise to come and find you – and deliver it.'

'Yes, and thank you,' said Mr Bold. 'But what's the message?'

Hector fluffed up his feathers. 'Imamu said to tell you that she is coming to visit.'

Chapter

Imamu was coming to VISIT!

Having stood up with surprise,
Mr Bold now had to sit down
with surprise. He was panting
a bit with SHOCK and Mrs Bold
fanned him with her apron
while Mr McNumpty
thought it best to
make everyone a
nice cup of tea.
The twins rushed
round to their
friend Minnie's

house to tell her the exciting news. The grandma they had always longed to meet was coming to stay!

Mr Bold began to pace the room. He had so many questions flying round his head. How was Imamu going to get to England? How would she know where they lived? Was she going to pretend to be a human too? When would she arrive? Was she staying for good, or planning to return to Africa?

But Hector didn't know any of the answers. Soon after his conversation with Imamu, he had wished her luck and set off on his long flight for England. He didn't have any other details for the Bolds.

This is rather exciting so far, don't you agree? I'm on the edge of my seat just writing it, and I'm not particularly comfortable, I don't mind telling you. I only hope this story calms down soon. But really – hyenas, a cuckoo, fleas even! You really get your money's worth with a Bolds book, if I do say so myself.

Not to mention the charming drawings by David Roberts. I sometimes put something or someone into the story just because I know he'll enjoy drawing it. It's my book after all, so I can do as I please. Do you remember Fifi Lampadaire, the singing French poodle from *The Bolds to the Rescue*? She was one of his favourites. As was Sheila the crocodile from the same book. And it's funny I should mention her, because Sheila is about to reappear in this book too. David *will* be pleased.

So here goes.

According to my sources, Imamu had a lot to think about after she first met Hector. Talking to the cuckoo about her lost pup had awakened a dormant longing to see Spot once more. Sometime before, she remembered, he had fallen in love with another hyena called Sue and then, quite suddenly, they had seized an opportunity to start a new life in England.

She would never forget the morning they had rushed into the den to tell her of their plans. A human couple called Mr and Mrs

Bold, on their honeymoon at the nearby Safari Lodge, had foolishly gone for a swim in a lake and been eaten by a crocodile. Spot and Sue had discovered Mr and Mrs Bold's clothes, together with a rucksack containing their passports, plane tickets and keys to their home in England: 41 Fairfield Road, Teddington. Spot had informed his mother that he was going to go and live in England as a human – and then he and Sue were gone, and Imamu

hadn't heard from them again. How could she? You can hardly send a postcard to a wild hyena, can you?

Then, a while later, word spread around the animals in that particular area of the Serengeti that there was a crocodile in the vicinity who wanted to have a word with Imamu. And can you believe it, but that crocodile was Sheila!

Sheila, as you might know, had been hatched in the sewers of Teddington and had swum up through the toilet of 41 Fairfield Road. The Bolds welcomed her into their home and taught her how to walk and talk and behave like a human. But life in Fairfield Road wasn't for her and she'd longed for a life in the wild. In the end the Bolds, with the help of Fifi the French poodle, had helped Sheila get to Africa in a daring plan. You can read all about this in *The Bolds to the Rescue*.

Now Sheila was blissfully happy living as a wild crocodile but had thought it might be kind to find the Bolds' clan and tell them how well Fred and Amelia were doing.

Sheila had swum up and down the Nile for months, asking every animal she met if they knew the whereabouts of Mr and Mrs Bolds' families, until finally she struck lucky. A chatty water buffalo told her she had heard about a hyena who had moved to England. His mother was called Imamu and she lived nearby. So the buffalo said she'd ask Imamu to meet Sheila just around the next bend in the river the following evening.

Sheila and Imamu met as arranged and Sheila told the hyena all about her long-lost son and how he lived happily in Teddington with his wife and children and how he had a job writing jokes for Christmas crackers.

67

But much to Sheila's surprise, the hyena wasn't pleased with the news. In fact, she was furious.

Imamu had raised her pup to be a rough, tough hyena. She had rather assumed that he would arrive in England disguised as a human but quickly go back to his hyena ways: perhaps live in a forest and hunt for his own food. The thought of her Spot still walking around on his hind legs, wearing human clothes and saying 'please' and 'thank you' made her bare her teeth with anger – and shame.

Then she thought of her grandchildren, the twins. How she longed to meet them! She did not, at all, like the idea that 'Betty' and 'Bobby' (what silly, unhyena-ish names!) were being raised as humans with their tails tucked away. But there was little she could do about it from Africa. She needed to go to England

and give her son a good talking-to. And make sure that her grandchildren knew about their hyena heritage and were PROUD of it – instead of pretending to be something they weren't.

'I'm grateful to you for telling me all this, Sheila,' said Imamu. 'But now I really feel I must go and see what's happening for myself.'

Sheila tried to convince her that there really was no need and that Spot and Sue seemed very happy with their new life.

However Imamu had made up her mind.

But just how could she go and visit? It was so very far away and she was a wild animal. A hopeless situation. Imamu spent a long time chewing over the dilemma. No solution seemed possible.

Then one day she had a very good idea and a plan began to form . . .

Chapter 6

One evening, in Teddington, a few weeks after Hector had visited the Bolds, Mrs Bold was drying the twins' tails with a hairdryer after their bath and Mr Bold was making them laugh with some funny jokes.

Why can't dogs drive?
Because they can't find a barking space!
Why did the belt go to jail?
Because he held up a pair of trousers!
What kind of shoes do frogs wear?
Open-toad!

'Time for bed now, children!' announced Mrs Bold.

'When will Grandma be coming to visit?' asked Betty, as she did **every** night. 'Will we see her tomorrow?'

'I'm afraid we don't know, Betty,' said her mother. 'We've heard nothing since Hector gave us the message.'

Betty and her brother looked very sad, so Fred decided to tell one more joke.

Why did Grandma put wheels on her rocking chair?

Because she wanted to rock and roll!

Betty and Bobby couldn't help but laugh as they climbed into their beds.

'But Grandma *will* come and see us soon, won't she?' asked Bobby. 'I've heard the children at school talking about their grandmas and I really want one too. Grandmas give you sweets, let you stay up late and knit you scarves for Christmas.'

'Well, I'm not sure about that,' said Mr Bold. 'All I can say is that if Grandma said she was going to come and visit, then she will.'

That did the trick and the twins were soon fast asleep with big smiles on their hairy faces. Their parents gave them each a gentle kiss on the forehead, turned the lights out and went downstairs to watch the evening news with Uncle Tony, a mug of cocoa in each of their paws.

'And finally, there are unconfirmed reports of an unusual animal seen on the loose in the West London area,' said a grim-faced newsreader. Suddenly on the screen was a blurry photograph of a creature taken at night on a mobile phone. 'Eyewitnesses say that a hyena-like animal with wild eyes has been seen foraging for food in dustbins at several locations in the West London suburb of Osterley. Our reporter Paul Black is live from the area.'

Mr Bold gasped. 'Listen, Amelia!' He turned up the volume.

On the TV, a stocky, bearded roving reporter was clutching a microphone. Behind him were several police vans with their blue lights flashing. 'I'm here with local resident

Marjorie Shaw. Talk us through exactly what you saw, Marjorie,' Paul said in a regional accent.

Marjorie, a worried-looking middle-aged lady, dabbed her eyes with a tissue. 'I heard a lot of noise from the front garden where the bins are. I opened my front door and there it was. A big, hairy thing with mad red eyes.'

'What was it doing?' asked Paul.

'Eating a dirty nappy,' said Marjorie. 'I mean, that's not normal, is it?'

Paul grimaced. 'No, it certainly isn't. I've never seen anything like that, and I come from Hull. Are you sure it wasn't a fox?'

'Oh, definitely not, no!' said Marjorie. 'It was bigger. Dirty grey, with spots down its back.

And a big mouth, drooling – teeth . . . Oh, it was 'orrible!'

'And did the creature see you?'

'Oh yes. Stared right through me, bold as brass. Then ran across the road and disappeared in the direction of Brentford.'

The reporter turned back to the camera. 'So there we have it. Some sort of wild animal is bringing terror onto the streets here. Armed police are on the scene and residents are being told to stay indoors with their windows locked. They're really really scared. This is Paul Black, Syon Lane, Osterley. Back to you in the studio.'

'She's here!' said Fred. 'Oh my goodness!'

'It *must* be her!' agreed Amelia. 'I wonder

how on earth she got to England, though?'

'My mother is a very determined hyena,' said Fred.

'Yes, I remember,' said his wife.

'And a very good-looking one, if that photo's anything to go by,' muttered old Uncle Tony.

Fred gave him a look.

'But how will she find her way to our street with armed police searching for her?' Amelia continued.

'Don't worry about that,' said Fred confidently. 'She has managed the first five thousand miles. It's just a hop and a skip from Osterley to Teddington.'

'But the police are after her, Fred!'

'Hyenas can creep up on a pride of lions unnoticed, remember. Who do you think are cleverer? Hyenas or police officers?'

'Oh, hyenas, definitely,' said Amelia after a moment's thought.

'Exactly,' said Fred. 'Oh, Mum! I can't wait to see you!'

It was very difficult for Mr and Mrs Bold to sleep that night. Fred kept getting up and peering through the curtains to see if there was any sign of his mother in the deserted Fairfield Road. But all was quiet and the pair eventually fell into a restless sleep.

Chapter

The next morning, to prevent the twins getting too excited, Mr and Mrs Bold didn't tell them about the item on the news and their firm conviction that Grandma's visit was imminent. They were careful not to turn on the radio or TV, and Mrs Bold took them to school as usual. If Grandma arrived it would be a wonderful *surprise* when they got home. If she didn't, then they wouldn't be disappointed.

'I wonder if I should work from home today?' Mr Bold asked his wife.

'Yes, dear,' said Mrs Bold. 'Good idea.

Your mother could arrive at any moment. I'm busy making a new hat for my market stall. I found an old toilet seat and some plastic pipes in a skip down the road and I'm going to create something very special.'

'I'm working on some new knock-knock jokes,' replied Fred.

'Try a couple out on me then,' said Amelia.

'That's enough, Fred,' chortled Amelia. 'I must get on with my hat.'

'Yes,' agreed Fred. 'What an exciting day this is!'

So Mr Bold sat at the kitchen table with his notepad, and Amelia got on with her hat-making. This creation was shaping up to be one of her best: with the help of some chicken wire, the toilet seat was raised above her head like a sort of halo. The lid could be lifted up, if desired, to create a sunshade while the plastic piping (which she had covered with glitter), curved around, pointing upwards. The whole creation was then finished off with a bright bunch of yellow plastic chrysanthemums sprouting cheerily from the end of the pipes.

'Splendid!' said Mrs Bold to herself, turning

her head from side to side and admiring her reflection in the mirror. 'Funny, original and very, very unusual, if I say so myself! I think I deserve a nice cup of tea now.'

But before she had a chance to remove the hat and put it on its stand, the doorbell rang. Amelia stopped and sniffed the air . . . Yes, she could definitely smell hyena. And, she was sure, a faint whiff of zebra too!

Then came a frantic knock at the door.

'Fred!' cried Mrs Bold. 'There's someone at the door!'

Mr Bold rushed into the hallway, took a deep breath and answered the door.

There before him appeared to be a large shrub, about a metre tall. The shrub trembled slightly.

'Er, hello?' said Fred, baffled.

'Let me in. It's your mother!' hissed the shrub.

Fred gasped and opened the door wide.

The green bush shot into the hall. 'Close the door, Spot, quick!' As soon as the door was

86

closed, the branches of the shrub cracked and splintered, a furry leg appeared, then another, then some round, furry ears and a snout. Finally the rest of the bush landed on the floor and there, bedraggled, panting, covered in leaves and looking a little bewildered, was someone unmistakeable – his mother!

'Mum!' cried Fred, throwing his arms around her. 'I can't *believe* you're here!' He could hardly speak for crying.

His mother hugged him back, but then pulled away quickly. 'Is it really you, Spot?'

She peered at Fred, looking him up and down. 'We hyenas don't hug each other.' She circled Fred on all fours, before pushing her snout towards his bottom. 'Yes,' she said, after a few sniffs. 'That's my boy!' She sounded relieved. 'Under the smell of soap and washing powder, it really is you!' She then nipped him on the back of the neck before rising up on her hind legs and smothering him, pulling him onto the floor where she began to wrestle him playfully, biting and licking and making soft, throaty growls of pleasure and the occasional high-pitched cackle. 'This is how a hyena greets her son! Never mind hugging and kissing, you big silly!'

It had been a long time since Fred had played rough and tumble with another hyena, as he used to do when he lived wild and free with the rest of the hyena clan. Since they had arrived in England, he and Mrs Bold had been very careful not to draw attention to themselves. The Bold family showed affection to each other, of course, but they had learned to do it in the human style. Bottom sniffing was for special occasions only.

But Fred's mother smelled of grass and mud and decidedly unwashed hyena! And it was wonderful! These were smells he and Amelia carefully scrubbed away every day. Now his skin tingled and his eyes shone with natural, animal joy. Fred and Imamu were lying, sprawled on their backs, snout to snout, still in the hallway.

'Mum! Mum!' he repeated. 'This is just,

well, amazing! I thought I would never see you again. However did you get here? I can't wait for you to meet Bobby and Betty, our twins.'

The kitchen door opened and there stood Amelia, still wearing her toilet-seat hat.

'Hello!' she said.

Imamu jumped up and crouched in the corner.

'It's all right, Mum!' laughed Fred. 'It's Amelia, my wife.'

Imamu continued to growl, her eyes focused on the toilet seat.

'Oh, sorry, Mum, of course you know Amelia better as Sue,' corrected Mr Bold.

Amelia removed her hat and placed it on the console table. Imamu slowly moved towards Mrs Bold, sniffing suspiciously.

'It's wonderful to see you again, Imamu,' said Amelia cautiously.

Imamu wasn't quite sure until she'd had a close sniff of the back of Mrs Bold's skirt. Then she jumped up and repeated the greeting she had done with Fred: neck nipping, jumping and wrestling to the ground. Mrs Bold's hyena instincts took over and she couldn't help but join in. She continued until the sound of ripping fabric pulled her to her senses.

'My blouse!' she shrieked, alarmed. 'I only got this

last week!' She jumped up and dusted herself down, looking at the large hole that had appeared in her new silk summer blouse.

Imamu pulled away and moved a metre or so back, looking from Fred to Amelia with a strange mixture of delight and horror. She shook her head, as if trying to wake herself up from a disturbing dream.

'This is worse than I thought,' she said finally.

'What is?' asked Fred.

'You. Both of you. Look at you, dressed up in suits and skirts. Smelling of flowers and deodorant. What is going on?'

'We live as humans now,' stated Amelia. 'It is important that we blend in with everyone else.'

'Mum,' said Fred. 'This is our new life. We *have* to live by human rules.'

'But you are hyenas!' said Imamu, bewildered. 'You should be *proud* of that. No hyena I've ever met wears clothes or silly hats made out of toilet seats. Or greets their mother with a polite hug. We hyenas are rough and ready! We bite and wrestle and fight! We are the true rulers of the Serengeti. How can you suppress all of this, demean yourselves by tottering around on your hind legs and covering up your true nature? Eh?' Imamu shook her head. 'I love you, Spot. I love you too, Sue. But this is a sorry sight.'

There was a long uncomfortable pause.

Eventually Mrs Bold spoke. 'I expect you're hungry. Food will make you feel better. Would you like a sandwich? Or maybe some smoked salmon with scrambled egg?'

Imamu's eyes looked even sadder. 'Sandwich? Smoked salmon? Oh dear. Hyenas eat meat. Raw meat, dripping with blood and preferably still with a pulse.'

Mrs Bold chuckled a little uncomfortably. 'Yes, I know. It took us a while to get used to the change in diet too. I'll give you the eggs raw. And I've got some mince. I guess you won't want it on a tray with a knife and fork?'

'No thanks,' said Imamu, following Mrs Bold to the fridge. The moment the door was opened Imamu dived in, eating anything she could find and growling contentedly at the same time.

Mr and Mrs Bold smiled indulgently. This, after all, was how they had once gone about meal times. They quite understood.

Once Fred's mother had had enough to eat, Fred and Amelia showed Imamu around the house before they all settled in the lounge. Mr and Mrs Bold sat on the sofa while Imamu sprawled on the rug, licking her paws.

'So, Mum,' said Mr Bold. 'There is so much I want to know. How is everyone back home? And how did you manage to come all this way?'

Imamu looked at him lovingly. 'A mother's love can overcome *any* obstacle, son,' she said. 'But it wasn't easy.' She paused to start chewing the rug.

'Er, best not to do that . . . it's new,' said Mrs Bold.

'Beg your pardon,' said Imamu. 'Hyenas like to chew things to clean their teeth after a meal.'

'Would you like a toothbrush?' suggested Fred. 'We have a spare one somewhere?' But one look at his mother made it clear a toothbrush would not be required.

'One day,' Imamu began, 'I met a crocodile on the banks of the Nile. Her name was Sheila.'

'Ah!' said Fred.

'Our old lodger!' said Mrs Bold. 'How is she?'

'Very well indeed. Swimming up and down the Nile, free as a, er, crocodile. She said you'd both been very kind to her, did your best to teach her how to live like a human: walk on her hind legs, wear clothes and so on. But she'd longed for the life of a wild crocodile, so you'd helped smuggle her on board a cruise ship disguised as a handbag. From there she reached the Nile and eventually met me. She told me where you live. And, er, how.' Imamu looked pityingly at Fred. 'And I wasn't very impressed. Hard to believe you are hyenas at all!'

Fred looked pleased. 'Yes, Mum. That's the idea.'

'Hmmm,' said Imamu. 'But then Sheila told me I have two grandchildren. Grandchildren I've never met!'

'Bobby and Betty,' said Mrs Bold proudly.

'Rather unhyena-ish names,' muttered Imamu.

'They will be so excited to meet you,' continued Mrs Bold.

'They'll be home from school soon,' added Fred.

'School, eh?' tutted Imamu. 'Fancy!'

'They're adorable,' said Mrs Bold, pointing to a photo of the twins, framed, on the mantelpiece.

Imamu got up for a closer look. 'Sweet,' agreed Imamu. 'But they could do with dirtying up a bit. Hyenas like to roll in the mud once in a while. Keeps the mosquitos away.'

'We dont have much trouble with mosquitos in Teddington,' pointed out Mr Bold.

'And not much mud allowed either, I don't suppose,' observed Imamu. 'All neat flower beds and pavements swept every week.'

Fred nodded. 'True,' he said. 'But there's plenty of mud in Bushy Park when it rains. And we do all like to play in the puddles if no one is looking.'

'Wild and crazy!' said Imamu, a hint of

100

sarcasm in her voice. 'Sheila the crocodile told me how, once in a while, you all allow a hint of your real selves to emerge.'

'Oh yes,' said Mrs Bold. 'Every Tuesday evening we have a grooming session. We pull the curtains and then the whole family has a good old scratch and rub and gets rid of any fleas.'

'Goodness!' said Imamu, rolling her eyes. 'You'll be killing flies with your bare hands next, if you're not careful.'

The Bolds let the comment pass. 'But please do go on with telling us how you got here,' pleaded Mrs Bold. 'I'm desperate to know.'

And so too are you, I imagine. Very well, I won't keep you in suspense any longer.

Chapter

Imamu settled back on her haunches and began her incredible tale.

'Much as I longed to see my son Spot again—'

'Fred!' interrupted Mr Bold. 'I'm called Fred now.'

'If you say so, Spot,' said his mother. 'As much as I wanted to see you, it was the thought of my two grandchildren – grandchildren I had never met – that made me really decide I had to come to England. It seemed impossible at first, but we hyenas are very determined. And very clever. Night and day I tried to think of a plan. And then finally I had an idea. Do you remember Dolores, the ostrich? Lived on the plains near us?'

Mr and Mrs Bold nodded immediately.

'Yes! A lovely bird,' said Mrs Bold. 'Beautiful feathers and a very long neck, as I recall.'

'That's her,' confirmed Imamu. 'Well, she disappeared a while ago, and according to her mother, she got a job at Kilimanjaro airport. In disguise as a human, of course.'

The Bolds nodded knowingly.

'But she visits her mother once a fortnight. I asked her to have a word with Dolores to see if there was any way she could get me onto a flight to England.'

'Good old Dolores, she was always very helpful,' remembered Fred.

'Indeed she was,' said Imamu. 'A few weeks later Dolores's mother came running towards me, most excited. She told me that several zebras were being held in crates ready to be flown over here to England as part of a conservation breeding programme.'

'Poor zebras!' said Mrs Bold.

'That's what I said,' agreed Imamu. 'But apparently the zebras were rather keen. They too wanted a new life in England, much like yourselves. They were to live safely in a luxurious, spacious park, get all their food and veterinary needs provided, and all they had to do was have the occasional baby!'

'Well, if you put it like that,' pondered Mr Bold, 'I rather tend to agree!'

'So Dolores had a plan. I met her at the airport perimeter fence the evening before the zebras' flight. Dolores knew of a back entrance. She was always clever like that. In the middle of the night she sneaked me into their crate where I hid under a pile of straw.'

'Didn't the zebras scream and shout?' asked Fred.

'No. Dolores had a word beforehand and they understood. I'd promised not to nibble them. Besides, there were five of them. A lot of hooves . . . I was a bit outnumbered.'

'Wow, what an adventure!' said Mrs Bold. 'And that explains the vague whiff of zebra I smelled when you arrived.'

'Yes, Sue, it would do,' replied Imamu. 'Anyway, I soon felt the crate being lifted up and rolled onto the plane, followed by some awful, loud whirring sounds.'

'That'd be the engines of the aeroplane starting up,' explained Fred. 'Deafening, isn't it?'

'I buried my head in the straw and didn't open my eyes until we got to Heathrow.'

'So what did you do then?'

'Dolores told me that it was up to *me* how I escaped, once in England. She couldn't help me. She had no "contacts". So I stayed where I was until the crate was moved to the animal quarantine reception area. Eventually some humans came and opened the crate and led the zebras away. I thought it best to stay hidden in the straw. The crate was then moved, I think into some kind of yard. When it was quiet and dark I chewed my way through the crate. I found some giant metal bins and climbed inside. There was food there.

RUBBISH

Stale and smelly, but I had to eat. And I drank from puddles, always hiding in the shadows or burrowing underneath outbuildings, terrified that I'd be seen. Three days I spent there, trying to work out my escape. It wasn't possible to climb fences or dig underneath them. For a start they were electric and there were cameras everywhere. But there was a gate that occasionally opened to allow vehicles through. I realised that I had struck lucky. This was a gate far away from the rest of the terminal. Part of a special VIP suite. The food in the bins there was of a much higher quality. I tucked into roasted tortilla chips cooked in rice bran oil, yellowtail tuna sashimi and diced, fresh papaya drizzled with dairy-free almond cream.'

'Delicious!' said Mrs Bold.

'Not really my thing,' said Imamu

dismissively. 'But at least the sashimi was raw. I stayed for a while, building up my strength. Then I saw my opportunity. A group called the . . . now, let me see if I can remember . . . Kashcows, or something, had just flown in from Los Angeles.'

'Not Kym Kashcow and her family?!' said Fred. 'They're very famous, though I'm not really sure what for.'

'Yes, that's them!' replied Imamu. 'Very sulky lot. Anyway, they had a whole fleet of cars waiting at the gate to whisk them away. There was a big car, like a Land Rover – we have those in Africa too – but this one was bigger and shinier. The number plate said KYM 1.'

'Kym Kashcow's private car!' shrieked Mrs Bold.

'Whatever,' said Imamu with a wave of her paw. 'It stopped for ages to load up all of her luggage. All matching. There was so much of it, a trailer was attached to the back. Then when the important woman emerged from the private celebrity suite—'

'That would be Kym!' said Fred knowingly.

'– the people loading the luggage had to stop and turn away. She doesn't like being looked at, apparently. I realised now was my chance. I jumped into the back of the trailer. A few minutes later we were off, out through the gates with me hidden amongst a load of suitcases. As we sped through the streets I realised that I was still a bit peckish. The cases smelled lovely, so I passed the time by chewing through the delicious leather bags. Then, when we stopped for a while at some traffic lights, I jumped out of the trailer and ran for cover in someone's back garden. A place called Osterley.'

'We saw that on the news!' cried Fred. 'You were seen by some bins, eating a dirty nappy!'

'Not one of my proudest moments,' said his mother.

'So how did you get from Osterley to Teddington?' asked Amelia, aghast at all she had heard.

'I found myself in Syon Park. A lot of trees and plants there. I disguised myself. Quite easy to move around amongst humans if you look like a shrub. As long as you don't move quickly and draw attention to yourself. I hopped on a couple of buses. The number sixty-five to Kingston, then the two-eight-one to Teddington.'

There was a stunned silence. 'So, to be clear, you hid in a crate full of zebras from Kilimanjaro to Heathrow, then sailed through airport security with Kym Kashcow and got on a bus to Teddington disguised as a shrub?' asked Mrs Bold, her eyes wide with wonderment.

'That's about the size of it,' said Imamu, nodding. 'All true, I promise you. Now. When can I meet my grandchildren?'

Chapter

While all of this was going on at home, the twins were having a rather eventful time at school that day. They never meant to be naughty but it seemed they got into trouble quite a lot nevertheless. Laughing or being silly were the usual reasons, although eating pencils and jumping from one desk to another were also not popular with teachers.

So when Mrs Bold arrived at school to pick up Bobby and Betty, she wasn't that surprised to be told they were in the headteacher's office yet again.

'Oh dear,' she said to herself. 'I wonder what they've done ᴎOW?'

There was a new headteacher at the school that term, called Mrs Dobson. She had a nice friendly face, with a generous chin and a mop of white hair.

'Come in!' she **boomed** in a deep, lived-in voice when Amelia knocked on the door.

Once inside, Mrs Bold saw the twins were sitting, giggling, on the window seat. Mrs Dobson strode towards Mrs Bold and shook her hand vigorously. 'Ah, Mrs Bold. Sorry to call you in to my office, but I thought I should have a word with you about Betty and Bobby's behaviour today . . .'

Mrs Bold smiled at her children. 'Hello!' she beamed. 'In trouble again?'

The twins nodded, looking surprisingly pleased with themselves.

'Well,' said Mrs Dobson, easing herself into her swivel chair behind the desk. 'There was an incident in the playground during afternoon break involving a pigeon . . .'

The twins began to giggle and Mrs Bold gave them a stern look. 'Oh dear, I'm sorry to

hear that, Mrs Dobson. They've never been keen on birds, ever since a seagull swooped down on them in their pram when they were still babies. I'm sure it won't happen again.' Amelia stood up. 'Is there anything else?'

'The pigeon didn't swoop down on them, Mrs Bold,' said Mrs Dobson, lowering her chin and her voice. 'The twins swooped down on the pigeon . . .'

Mrs Bold looked at Bobby and Betty. 'Ha, ha!' she laughed. 'Do tell me more, Mrs Dobson.'

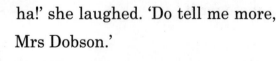

'It all happened very quickly, I'm told. By the time *I* arrived, there were only a few feathers left.'

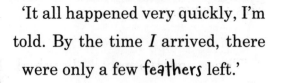

'You mean . . . ?'

'Yes, I'm afraid so, Mrs Bold. Betty and Bobby ate the poor thing.'

There was a pause while Mrs Bold pondered how to respond. 'Er, I see,' she said at last. Another pause. 'I think I can explain this to you, Mrs Dobson. The twins, you see, didn't have any breakfast this morning. My fault entirely. I, er, ran out of time. Overslept. They would have been unusually peckish. And we had pigeon for lunch at a restaurant in Richmond on Sunday. They must have got a taste for it.'

'But raw pigeon? Unplucked?' said Mrs Dobson.

'These gastro-pubs!' laughed Mrs Bold. 'I don't know how they get away with it!'

Mrs Dobson quietly considered Mrs Bold's

119

explanation for a moment. 'I would like your reassurance that this unpleasantness won't be repeated, Mrs Bold. It was a little too feral for our school.'

'I can assure you that Bobby and Betty will eat no more pigeons during break time,' said Mrs Bold confidently. 'Will you, children?'

'No, we promise,' said Betty and Bobby in unison.

'What about sparrows?' asked Bobby.

'No birds of any kind!' clarified Mrs Bold, before turning back to the headteacher. 'We are very sorry, Mrs Dobson.'

'Then I think we can say that is an end to the matter,' said Mrs Dobson, rising up from her chair and giving Mrs Bold's hand another firm shake. As she felt the unusual contours of Mrs Bold's paw she looked momentarily confused, and glanced down at it, but Amelia sensed her hesitancy and pulled away, placing her suspicious-looking mitt firmly behind her back.

'Such spirited children!' she laughed. 'I expect they'll make a name for themselves one day. A credit to us Bolds and the school too! Come on, kids. Let's get you home. There is a surprise waiting for you.'

Bobby and Betty guessed immediately what it might be, and leaped to their feet, trying their best not to jump up and down with excitement.

Once in the back of the blue Honda, seat belts fastened, they wanted to know:

'Has Grandma arrived?'

'Yes, dears, she has,' replied Mrs Bold.

'Yay!' said Betty.

'I can't wait!' said Bobby.

'But listen, children,' said Mrs Bold, glancing at her excited pups in the rear-view mirror and trying her best to be serious. 'You really *mustn't eat* any more pigeons. At least, not in the playground, do you understand? We mustn't have our secret discovered.'

'Sorry, Mum,' said Betty.

'I don't know what happened,' explained Bobby. 'One minute I was playing hopscotch and the next minute I was chowing down on a pigeon. It just happened so quickly.'

'Your hyena hunting instinct,' replied their mother knowingly. 'But you must fight against it, dears. We will get into trouble otherwise.'

'Sorry, Mum,' said Bobby sincerely.

'I know you didn't mean it,' said Mrs Bold. 'Let's forget about that. Grandma is waiting!'

Chapter

The twins' first meeting with their grandma was very emotional. As soon as the car was parked outside 41 Fairfield Road, they jumped out and raced up the path. Mr Bold opened the door and the twins ran to Imamu, yelping and whooping with joy. Mrs Bold ran in behind them and Mr Bold shut the door quickly, to make sure none of the neighbours saw the display of animal behaviour taking place.

'Grandma! Grandma!' cried the twins.

Imamu rolled on her back, allowing her grandchildren to pounce on her, squealing

and yelping with joy. She playfully nipped and nuzzled the two young pups, pushing them away with her big paws only for them to leap back on top of her in a glorious hyena bundle of affection and bonding. Bobby and Betty licked and kissed their never-before-seen grandma, and cries of delight and love rose through the air from all three of them.

Fred and Amelia stood back and watched,

simultaneously thrilled that their young pups were hyenas, bold and brave, but at the same time a little concerned that the wild animal noises they were making might disturb the other residents in Fairfield Road.

The excitement eventually died down. The twins phoned and invited their best friend Minnie over to meet their grandma. Imamu was a little wary of meeting a human child, and indeed Minnie was a little nervous too. It's not often you go to meet your friends' naked hairy grandmother. But Minnie's kind, gentle nature soon won Imamu over.

'I know you are a good friend to my grandchildren,' said Imamu. 'And you keep their secret!'

'Oh yes,' nodded Minnie. 'I would never tell tales – or even tails!'

Just then the door opened and in wandered Uncle Tony (with Miranda tucked inside his jacket) and Mr McNumpty, back from a trip to Teddington High Street and the library. They were deep in conversation, and at first didn't see Imamu sitting on the rug – until she began to growl.

'It's all right, Mum. Uncle Tony is one of *us*. We rescued him from the safari park nearby. And this is our next-door neighbour, Mr McNumpty.'

Imamu slowly approached Tony and Nigel,

sniffing suspiciously. Her tail wagged with delight as she perused Uncle Tony. What a handsome devil – even if he was wearing a silly flat cap and tracksuit. Uncle Tony grinned at Imamu and she wagged her tail in response. 'Pleased to meet you, my dear,' said Uncle Tony.

But Imamu wasn't so sure about Mr McNumpty, and sat back down on her haunches. 'I've never seen one of you before,' she said.

'I'm a grizzly bear,' said Mr McNumpty, doffing his hat. 'How do you do?'

It wasn't until dinnertime, however, that problems with the Bolds' visitor started to appear. Mrs Bold cooked a nice chicken casserole with cauliflower cheese and the Bolds family sat at the table as usual to eat it. But Imamu thought this was silly behaviour. She insisted on eating off the floor – and furthermore wouldn't allow Mrs Bold to cook her piece of chicken.

Amelia quite understood that Imamu was a wild hyena and so she did as her mother-in-law asked. But the twins looked enviously at their granny.

'I'd like to eat my food raw and off the floor in future,' said Betty. 'It looks much nicer.'

'Yes, me too,' agreed Bobby. 'And no more plates or cutlery for us!'

'No, children,' said Mrs Bold. 'It wasn't easy teaching you table manners. They're very important to humans. And don't turn your fork over, Bobby.'

'Tastes much nicer like this, though,' said Imamu, speaking with her mouth full. Mrs Bold shot her husband a worried look.

'Now then!' said Fred. 'Your mother's right, kids. Manners matter! Which reminds me . . .'

After dinner there was another incident. The twins were enjoying their usual bubble-filled bath and a rousing chorus of 'Row, row, row your boat, merrily down the stream', when Imamu wandered into the bathroom. Without warning she suddenly leaped into the bath with the twins, splashing water all over the floor. The twins thought this was hilarious fun,

and all three jumped in and out of the bath, racing in circles around the upstairs floor of the house, soaking carpets, beds and furniture with warm soapy water. Imamu then showed the twins how to shake the water off instead of using a towel, not worrying about the spray all up the walls. Then into the bath again, then out and around and more shaking.

Mr and Mrs Bold ran upstairs to see what all the noise was about.

'Nooo!' cried Mrs Bold, looking in dismay at the wet footprints, wet carpets, beds and walls. 'You *can't* do that, children! Stop at once! Imamu, please – we aren't in Lake Victoria now! This is all going to take hours to clean up.'

'Sorry, Mum,' said the twins rather sheepishly. 'It was such fun we didn't stop to think about all the mess we were making.'

'But what's wrong with mess?' asked Imamu, genuinely confused.

'Well, er,' explained Fred, as he wrapped Bobby and Betty in fluffy towels and rubbed their backs. 'Mess is fun, I know. And it is all right sometimes. In the garden, for instance. But not in the house. Unless you're painting a picture and you've got special clothes on, like overalls, and newspaper on the floor.'

'Painting?' repeated Imamu, tilting her head to one side. 'What's that? And what are overalls?'

'Oh dear,' said Fred. 'The thing is, Mum, humans don't like mess. Only at certain times and places, like if they're playing football, or gardening, or if they live in Chatham. Bathtime is about getting clean, not making a mess.'

'But who cares what humans do?' asked Imamu, genuinely baffled.

'We do! We need to behave like humans,' said Amelia. 'Or our secret will get out and we'll be locked up or sent back to the Serengeti.'

Imamu shook her head sadly. 'Oh well. If *that's* what you want. I mean, Heaven forbid that you'd have to go back to the Serengeti and live like a normal hyena,' she said huffily.

'Now, Mother, Amelia didn't mean any offence,' said Mr Bold. 'The point we're trying to make is that we have a life here, a good life, and we don't want it to change.'

Imamu shrugged and moved over to the twins, nuzzling them affectionately before walking, head bowed, towards the stairs. 'It's just something I'm never going to understand. Clean. Dirty. What does it matter? What matters is having fun, I've always thought. It's what hyenas do. Or used to. Mind if I go for a snooze on the sofa? Or are you worried about me dribbling on your nice clean cushions and leaving a few hairs?' Imamu turned to leave but gave the twins a secret wink before she went downstairs for her rest.

As they were put to bed that evening the

twins were a little *subdued*.

'Come on, cheer up!' said Mr Bold.

'We're sad for Grandma,' said Betty. 'We love her so much, and she was only playing with us. She didn't mean any harm.'

'I know, dear – it's just going to take a bit of time for her to get used to our way of life. Let me cheer you both up with some jokes tonight, instead of a bedtime story.'

'Yes please,' said Bobby, settling under his duvet (that still had one or two damp patches on it).

Which birds steal soap from the bath?

Robber ducks!

Mrs Bold laughed along with the twins at Mr Bold's jokes. But at the back of her mind she was starting to worry. It was lovely having Imamu with them – she was part of the family, after all. But her wild ways were already rubbing off on the children. There was a distinct possibility that there could be trouble ahead.

And she was right.

Chapter

Luckily, animals – unlike humans – tend not to sulk (at least not for long) and Imamu was back to her cheerful self the next morning.

'Sorry about all the mess I made last night, Amelia,' she said to Mrs Bold, who was in the kitchen making breakfast.

'That's all right,' smiled Amelia. 'It took Fred and I a long time to adjust our behaviour when we first got here. And poor Uncle Tony *still* struggles. No harm done.'

'I've decided I mustn't be a nuisance.

I'm going to help you around the house from now on.'

'Really?' answered Mrs Bold, not quite sure how a wild hyena was going to help with domestic matters. There was a slight glint in Imamu's eyes too, which was somehow worrying.

'Oh yes, my dear daughter-in-law,' smiled Imamu. 'I'm going to start right away. What can I do to help?'

'Um. You could clean these dishes in the sink, I suppose,' said Amelia doubtfully. 'I left them in to soak overnight.'

Imamu, on all fours, couldn't reach the sink, but she leaped onto the draining board in a second and immediately started licking the dishes with her long pink tongue. 'I'll have them sorted in no time,' she said determinedly.

'Oh, I didn't imagine cleaning them like that,' said Amelia. 'We usually use washing-up liquid and a brush.'

'Much quicker this way,' pointed out Imamu. And it was true. Her rough tongue scoured its way through the burnt crusty bits on the casserole dish in no time before moving on to the Pyrex dish with a cheesy residue. Finished, she licked her lips. 'Surprisingly tasty! What shall I do to help you next, dear?'

Unconventional though this new dish-cleaning method was, it was certainly effective. And so cleverly hyena-ish! Mrs Bold made a mental note to cross Brillo pads off her shopping list.

'Well, I was about to go for my shower, then check that Bobby and Betty were dressed properly for school,' she said.

'Ah, yes, clothes,' said Imamu with a note of distaste in her voice. 'I can do that for you.'

Amelia looked worried. 'They are old enough to dress themselves, of course. But it's the business of their tails . . .' Mrs Bold's voice trailed away.

'What about their tails?' asked Imamu.

'We have to tape them down. With gaffer tape, you see.'

'Why is that?' Imamu looked genuinely confused.

'To keep them still,' explained Mrs Bold. 'Something moving about in their pants would be most suspicious.'

Imamu's eyes seemed to glint even more. 'Of course, I understand. You go for your shower and I'll check on the pups – or as you call them, kids.'

'It's quite tricky,' said Mrs Bold, unsure if this was wise. 'If you're not used to gaffer tape.'

'Don't worry, I'm sure I can manage,' said Imamu. 'Tape down the tails so they don't move. Easy. Leave it to me.'

So Mrs Bold did.

What would Imamu think about taping down her grandchildren's tails? Do you suppose she would think it was a good idea? Me neither.

As she went upstairs to the twins' bedroom, Imamu felt her own tail wagging, involuntarily, at the thought of seeing young Bobby and Betty. What a joyful feeling it was! She couldn't *imagine* having it tied down. How uncomfortable, how awful, how very wrong!

As humans, we don't have tails so it is hard to think of an equivalent. But imagine trying to stop yourself smiling. Or laughing. What a tricky business!

When Imamu went into the twins' bedroom they were almost dressed, but they had got distracted by jumping up and down on their beds to try and catch the lampshade, which was swinging tantalisingly from side to side.

Seeing something moving triggered Imamu's hunting instinct and she leaped into the air instantly, grabbing the lampshade between her teeth and growling. It came loose from the light fitting and she crunched it between her jaws. Bobby and Betty looked on in amazement, then rushed to join in the 'hunt'. Within seconds the lampshade had been destroyed – a few shreds of fabric in each hyena's mouth.

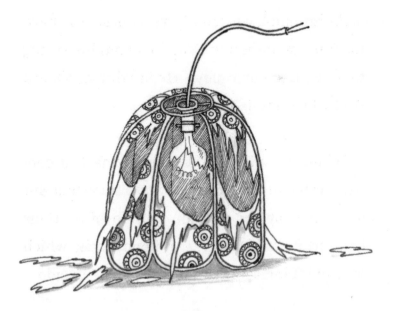

'Oops!' said Imamu. 'I expect we will get into trouble for that . . . Let's say it just fell apart, eh? Wear and tear. From the taste of it, it wasn't a quality product.'

The twins looked at each other.

'We really can't tell lies. Especially to Mum and Dad,' said Bobby.

'Quite right,' said their grandma. 'We'll just be honest and tell them *I* did it then. Ha, ha, ha! Now, apparently I need to tape down your tails so they don't move about while you're at this school place.'

Betty sighed. 'Yes,' she said. 'We hate it. Not school, but tying down our tails. But we can't control them, so they have to be kept still somehow. The gaffer tape is on the dressing table.'

Imamu picked up the tape and sneered at it, then looked affectionately at her two grandpups. 'But isn't it very uncomfortable?' she asked.

'To be honest, Grandma, yes it is,' said Betty. 'But there is no alternative.' Betty held the end of her tail and pulled it tight around her tummy. 'Ready,' she said with a sigh, bracing herself.

'Listen,' said Imamu. 'Let your tail go. Why not try a day at school without having your tails taped down? I don't think anyone will notice. Just make sure you don't go wagging them too frantically.

A gentle swishing and you'll get away with it,
I'm sure.'

'Really?!' exclaimed Bobby, delighted. 'That
would be so cool!'

'No gaffer tape!' cried Betty. 'Oh, yesss!
Thank you, Grandma!'

'I can't see the harm in it,' said Imamu,
smiling at her grandchildren indulgently.
'Your tails are yours and no one else's. What
you do with them is your own business. And
something that seems to have been forgotten
in this house is that you are hyenas, first and
foremost. The cleverest animals in all of Africa!
Don't let anyone tell you otherwise, my dears.'

An hour later the twins arrived at school, their tails free beneath their clothes for the first time ever. And it felt wonderful.

What could possibly go wrong, you might ask? Quite a lot as it happened. And fairly quickly.

Chapter

It was unfortunate for Bobby and Betty that Mrs Dobson was keeping a firm eye on them after the incident with the pigeon the previous day. She was at the school gates when they arrived that morning and she followed them into the cloakroom. When Bobby reached up to hang his coat on his peg she noticed something hairy peeping out from under his shorts. And as Betty reached down to pick up her satchel, a similar oddity appeared from under the hem of her skirt.

Mrs Dobson's eyes widened. She wasn't quite sure what she had seen, but she was

suspicious. She went back to her office where she sat at her desk for a good think. There was something very different about the Bold twins. She had thought so from the moment she first met them. Very pleasant, very helpful, but decidedly unusual. There were children of all shapes and sizes in her new school, it was true, but she had never met two children who laughed and giggled quite as much as Betty and Bobby Bold. And because they laughed so much, mouths wide open, heads thrown back, she couldn't help but have noticed how very pointed their teeth were . . . Then there were their ears: very round and rather hairy, and set high on the tops of their heads . . .

When she'd first met Mrs Bold she'd had a similar feeling. Something was amiss there, she was sure of it. But what? Mrs Dobson let out a big sigh. It takes all sorts to make a world and she wasn't there to judge. I mean, what would people think if they knew about her own son, she wondered. Shut up in his room all day, making strange noises, perched on top of the wardrobe and eating bananas. She loved him no matter what – but still, she knew that he was not what could be described as 'normal'.

Nevertheless, Mrs Dobson was sure she had glimpsed something peculiar in the school cloakroom that morning. It was probably just another one of the Bold twins' endless jokes. Something they had stuck onto their clothes to make everyone laugh, maybe. But even so she couldn't just ignore it. She was the headteacher, after all.

So Mrs Dobson decided to wander down the corridor to the twins' classroom and just check that all was well. When she got there she didn't go in, but peered through the glass. It was very quiet. A few sums were written on the board and the children were all hunched over their exercise books, concentrating. Well, not quite all the children. The Bolds weren't very keen on maths. And nor was their friend, Minnie. Betty and Bobby always sat next to each other at the front of the class (where the teacher could keep an eye on them, should they start being silly). Minnie was a few rows behind.

As Mrs Dobson watched, the class teacher turned her back on the children in order to write another sum on the board. The twins saw their opportunity and nimbly jumped onto their desks to turn and pull silly faces at Minnie. That is when Mrs Dobson saw the two furry appendages once more. Her view through the classroom door was very clear and direct. This time she knew exactly what they were.

Both Bobby and Betty had tails!

Real tails, for they twitched and swished, and were certainly not pretend ones tied to their waists.

Mrs Dobson rushed back to her office, trembling with shock. Everything made sense now – the teeth and ears, the unusual laugh, and now the tails. She had seen the news the other day too. An animal on the loose not far from Teddington. Yes, she was sure. These weren't humans. They were animals. And what's more, she thought they might be hyenas!

'Oh my!' she muttered to herself. 'Whatever can I do? Hyenas in my school! Supposing they bite one of the children? What about rabies? I'd get the sack! I wonder if I should call the police?' Mrs Dobson paced up and down her office. 'But wait. They are such a nice family. There is *nothing* in the rule book about hyenas. Oh dear, oh dear. Whatever is the right thing to do?'

A few minutes later she had made up her mind. She lifted the telephone and dialled.

'Mrs Bold? It is Mrs Dobson here at the

school. I wonder if you and Mr Bold could come in and see me rather urgently? No, the twins are fine – there hasn't been an accident or anything. I will explain when you get here. Yes, as soon as possible, please.'

Mrs Bold could tell from the headteacher's voice that something of importance was the matter, so she phoned Fred at the Christmas cracker factory and told him she'd had a call from the school.

'School, eh?' said Fred cheerily.

Why didn't the nose want to go to school?

He was tired of getting picked on!

'No, Fred, listen,' said Mrs Bold.

What did the pencil sharpener say to the pencil?

Stop going round in circles and get to the point!

'Fred, the headteacher said—'

What vegetables do librarians like?

Quiet peas!

'Not now, Fred.'

What do elves learn in school?

The elf-abet!

Mrs Bold knew Fred would go on and on with the jokes. She'd have to **shout** to stop him.

'FRED! LISTEN TO ME! WE HAVE TO GO TO THE SCHOOL URGENTLY! RIGHT NOW! DO YOU UNDERSTAND?!'

There was a pause on the other end of the phone.

'Oh. Right. The school, you say?'

'Yes, Fred,' said Mrs Bold, relieved. 'The headteacher called. She needs to see both of us, urgently. The twins are fine, but her voice was shaking.'

Oh dear. What's red and flies and wobbles at the same time?

A jelly-copter!

'Fred, STOP!' shouted Mrs Bold, even louder than before. 'Can you tell your boss it is an emergency and you have to leave work for a while? Meet me at the school gates in half an hour?'

Thirty minutes later Fred and Amelia were shown into Mrs Dobson's office.

'Thank you for coming in,' said Mrs Dobson. 'Please take a seat.' Her voice was quivering and she looked a little flushed. 'You will excuse me if I lock the door? What I need to speak to you about is a very delicate matter and we wouldn't want to be interrupted . . .' Without waiting for an answer she turned the key firmly, then sat behind her desk.

'Whatever is the matter, Mrs Dobson?' asked Amelia.

Mrs Dobson didn't answer immediately, but sat with her head in her hands and her eyes shut. Her mouth opened and closed but it was as if she couldn't find the words. Eventually she spoke.

'Mr and Mrs Bold, I need to ask you a rather unusual question. A question I've **never** asked any parent before.'

How do you make a milk shake?

Give it a good scare!

'No, it wasn't that,' said Mrs Dobson.

Why was the broom late?

He overswept!

'No,' said Mrs Dobson firmly, clearly more than a little put out by Mr Bold's irrelevant interjections.

'Fred, hush,' said Amelia. 'Mrs Dobson has something important to ask us.'

'Sorry,' said Fred. 'I couldn't help myself.'

There was silence again for a moment. Mr and Mrs Bold looked at Mrs Dobson expectantly. She looked from one to the other, cleared her voice, and then asked the question.

'Are you . . . hyenas?'

Chapter

Poor Mr and Mrs Bold looked at each other in horror and their jaws dropped open. This was the moment they'd been dreading ever since they left Africa. Had they actually, finally, been found out? Would this be the end of the wonderful lives they'd built for themselves?

Mrs Bold spoke first. 'Why do you ask that?' she said, trying to laugh it off. 'What a strange question.'

'Because I've seen Betty and Bobby's tails, Mrs Bold,' replied Mrs Dobson plainly.

Amelia's hand jumped to her mouth. 'Oh no,' she said.

'Oh yes,' said Mrs Dobson.

'How come they weren't taped down?' Mr Bold asked his wife.

'Your *mother* was supposed to do that this morning, Fred,' sighed Mrs Bold.

'So it is true, then?' said Mrs Dobson. 'There really are hyenas in my school.'

'Well, yes. It is true, sort of,' said Amelia. 'But—'

'You are a family of hyenas?' asked Mrs Dobson.

Mrs Bold took a deep breath. 'Yes, we are.

But we live like humans and we're no bother to anyone. Please don't tell on us. Please. We'll be locked up in a zoo somewhere or the children will be taken away from us. Please don't let that happen. Let us explain!'

Mrs Dobson shook her head. 'I–I–I've never heard of such a thing!' She stood up and paced around her office. 'Yes, you had better explain, because I find it very alarming! Hyenas? Here? In Teddington? You're not going to attack me, are you?'

'Heavens, no!' said Mrs Bold. 'We're very civilised. We don't scavenge or hunt any more and we know how to use cutlery and a toilet.'

Mrs Dobson looked a little more comfortable.

'We're really not so unusual,' said Mr Bold with a shrug.

'Aren't you?' said Mrs Dobson disbelievingly.

'We animals are cleverer than you humans think. Some of us live in the wild, some of us live in fields and woods and jungles. But not all of us. There are animals who have crossed over, Mrs Dobson. We live in houses, have jobs, drive cars. Some of us even work in schools.'

'As teachers?' questioned Mrs Dobson, the colour rising in her cheeks.

'Headteachers, even,' said Mrs Bold.

'We know of a koala bear at Eton,' said Mr Bold, lowering his voice.

'A chemistry professor at Cambridge is a particularly clever goat!' revealed Mrs Bold. 'So, you see, it's nothing to get in a fluster about. But usually humans never find out. You're too busy thinking of yourselves as the most intelligent species to notice *us* living among you.'

'So you're not trying to take over or anything?' asked Mrs Dobson, her tone more than a little suspicious.

'Not at all!' said Mrs Bold reassuringly. 'We like humans. We just want to improve our lot in life. Fred and I were living wild in the Serengeti. But an opportunity came along to live here and we took it. We love our new life. And Betty and Bobby have never known anything different.'

'That explains why they are always eating

pencils,' said Mrs Dobson, rubbing her chin.

'But they're good pups on the whole, aren't they?' pleaded Mrs Bold.

'Yes. When they're not being silly or making a snack out of pigeons.'

'Oh, Mrs Dobson, please don't tell. They'll end up in a zoo, or worse. We all will. You can come and visit our home. You'll see how clean and tidy it is. We live just like you do. You'd have no idea we are animals, I assure you.'

'I – I couldn't bear the thought of you all going to live in a zoo,' said Mrs Dobson. 'But this is such a lot to take in! Animals living as human beings . . . !'

'But we can. And we do. In fact, we're so good at it that my husband and I are known for helping *other* animals to live in the human world, if that's what they want.'

'We have a sort of open house policy,' added Mr Bold. 'We've helped lots and lots! A sheep who now works in childcare. A poodle who is a well-known cabaret singer, two horses whose landscape gardening skills are much sought after . . .'

'A wild boar who now runs an alcohol-free beer business,' continued Mrs Bold. 'A goose who does very well as a traffic warden.'

'And an otter who is now a very holy nun,' concluded Fred. 'We Bolds are not that unusual, after all!'

Mrs Dobson gazed at a framed photograph of her son on her desk. 'So tell me, Mr and Mrs Bold . . . if animals can live as humans, does that mean humans could live as animals too?'

Mr Bold looked at the photo. It was of a rather unhappy-looking young man with long unkempt hair. Curiously, his long arms almost touched the ground. Mr Bold glanced at his wife.

'We think *everyone* should be allowed to live any way they want to, Mrs Dobson.'

'Please, call me Margaret,' said Mrs Dobson. 'Then perhaps you can help me with something that has been a great worry to me for a very long time.'

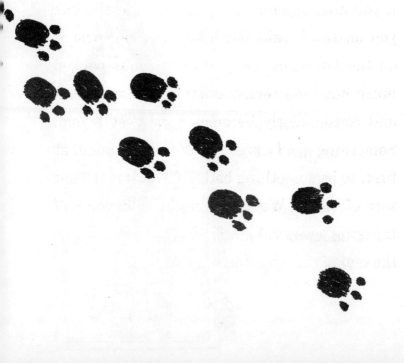

Chapter

Mrs Dobson finding out about the Bolds' true identity might seem like a terrible thing to happen. Disaster! But as I told you earlier: 'Everything happens for a reason.' Imagine if you miss the bus, for example, but the bus you missed breaks down and you sail past it on the later bus. Or you forget your packed lunch but then someone lets you share theirs and consequently becomes your best friend. Something good comes out of what seemed, at first, to be something bad. Fate! Karma! That sort of thing. Well, you might find yourself thinking, *everything happens for a reason*, by the end of this chapter. Just saying.

Now, first of all there's something you should know: it's never a good idea to leave a wild hyena at home alone in a semi-detached house. Mrs Bold had rushed out to the school in such a panic she didn't think about what Imamu would do to occupy herself. Uncle Tony asked her whether she fancied joining him in Bushy Park for an ice cream, but when she heard she'd have to dress up in Mrs Bold's clothes and walk on her hind legs, she quickly declined. So Uncle Tony went with Mr McNumpty instead.

Alone in the house, Imamu decided her teeth needed a good clean, so she looked around for a piece of wood to chew on. She couldn't find one, so had a pleasant gnaw of the kitchen counter and then the cupboard doors, which were surprisingly flimsy and not, as it turned out, very firmly attached. The dining-room curtains then fluttered in a breeze from the window, which ignited her hunting instincts once again, so a bit of a tug of war ensued. It's fair to say Imamu won. The curtains gave way to her superior strength in no time and came tumbling down, complete with the curtain rail. She leaped on them, growling, using her newly sharpened teeth to tear the fabric into shreds.

It then seemed a good idea to bury her 'prey', so a hole had to be dug. The carpet soon gave way, but the floorboards took a little longer. Down and down Imamu pawed, then dragged curtains, curtain rail and what was left of the kitchen cupboard doors into the freshly dug den. It was much harder work than at home in Africa, she noted.

A den there would then be camouflaged with branches and leaves. Imamu looked around. No branches, but she made do with the stuffing from the sofa (easily accessed with a few deft

strikes of her claws), the kitchen blinds and the laundry from the clothes horse. Eventually she sat back, panting, to admire her work. It wasn't perfect, she conceded, but it was a lot more homely than before – if home is the wild Serengeti plains, that is.

Just then there was the sound of a key in the front door. Amelia *will* be pleased, thought Imamu to herself.

As soon as Amelia entered the front door of 41 Fairfield Road she could smell trouble: a woody, earthy scent that wasn't there when she left.

'Imamu?' she called. 'Tony? Are you there?'

Imamu bounded into the hallway and greeted Amelia in the traditional hyena fashion – tail wagging, bottom sniffing and a spot of rough and tumble. Being a hyena herself, Amelia joined in, even if it meant her dress was pulled up around her armpits and her turban was rather squashed in the process.

'Yes, lovely to see you again,' said Amelia, brushing herself down and putting her turban back on. 'But tell me, why weren't the twins' tails taped down this morning? There has been a great deal of trouble. The headteacher – Mrs Dobson – saw their tails and now knows the truth about who we *really* are. And why can I smell wood and damp and sofa stuffing?'

'Oh,' said Imamu, waving her paw dismissively, 'no hyena should suffer the indignity of having his or her tail taped down with gaffer tape, I decided. Our tails are how we express ourselves. Free all tails! So I decided not to bother. As for the smell that your sensitive hyena nose has picked up on, come into the dining room and see . . . I've been busy!'

Mrs Bold entered the dining room and looked with dismay at the devastation. 'Oh, goodness me,' she said quietly. But despite herself, Mrs Bold's nostrils flared and she inhaled the lovely smell of freshly dug suburbia.

'Great, isn't it?' said Imamu. 'Almost like home!'

'Imamu, you have followed your instincts and done just what I would like to do sometimes.

But we can't live like this in Teddington. Humans wouldn't **understand**.'

Imamu looked crestfallen. She shook her head. 'No. I don't suppose they would. But I'm a hyena. I want my grandchildren to know what that **feels** like. Taping down their tails? It's not natural, Amelia! Living a neat and ordered life? **Ridiculous!**'

Amelia nodded knowingly. 'Humans are animals too. But there is something called "compromise" and another thing called "consideration". It is what humans are good at. This is how civilisation works. Otherwise it would be **chaos** everywhere.'

'So that is why humans say please and thank you? Why they flush their **poo** down a toilet in case the smell offends anyone? Why they smile when they really want to snarl?'

'Well, yes, I suppose so,' said Mrs Bold, busy thinking about how much it would cost to repair the kitchen cupboards and replace the curtains and carpet in the dining room.

Imamu sat down and sighed. 'Well, I'm not sure it's for me. I'm so pleased I came to see you, Fred and my grandchildren. I had a dream that I could persuade you all to come back to Africa with me. But I can tell that isn't going to happen. Your lives are here. I can see that now. But I must find a way to go back myself. With or without you all. Because this definitely isn't a life I can adapt to. You have seen the mess I made of your dining room . . . I'll only do it again if I'm here for too long. I will stay for a few more weeks and then I think I should be going, before I destroy your home.'

Amelia put a comforting paw on Imamu. 'Don't worry about it,' she said. 'Fred will put it all back how it was.'

'I am proud of my hyena self,' said Imamu with a shrug. 'I *can't* change. I don't want to, more to the point.'

'Hmmm,' said Mrs Bold. 'Nor should you. But something happened today, funnily enough, as a result of the twins' tails swinging freely. And I think you are going to be a great help in this matter. Please don't go home just yet.'

'How can *I*, a wild hyena visiting Teddington, possibly be of any help?' asked Imamu, genuinely baffled.

'Well,' said Mrs Bold, 'we are going to need your help with Mrs Dobson's son.'

'How come?'

'You know how we are hyenas, living as humans?'

'Yes,' said Imamu.

'You see, Jeffrey Dobson – a human – wants to live as a wild animal.'

'What sort of wild animal?'

'A chimpanzee.'

'You're kidding me?'

'No, I'm not. As a result of Mrs Dobson finding out about Bobby and Betty's tails, we had to confess the truth to the her. She was terribly shocked. As you'd expect.'

'Oh no,' said Imamu. 'She's not going to put you all in a zoo, is she?'

'Well, no. That's the strange thing. It was as if fate had brought us together – she told us about her son.'

Imamu gazed into space. 'Being a mother is difficult sometimes. When your children want a **different** sort of life from the one you had imagined for them, what can you do?'

Mrs Bold knew that Imamu was thinking about Fred and how far removed his life was from her own. She stroked Imamu's shoulder. 'I know,' she said softly. 'But I think we should try to help Mrs Dobson.'

'You mean, go to meet her monkey son?'

'Yes,' said Mrs Bold. 'And perhaps, if we can find a way, we can help Jeffrey to live his dream.'

'What does he want exactly?'

'To be a wild chimpanzee. Living in Africa.'

'Now that I *can* understand!' said Imamu, smiling for the first time in a few minutes. 'Perhaps, if I can't go home with my own son, I can go home with someone else's.'

As I said a few pages back – everything happens for a reason. Was I right, or was I right?

Chapter

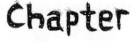

The next day was Saturday and the Bolds were going on an outing to Mrs Dobson's house: Mr and Mrs Bold, Bobby and Betty, Uncle Tony and Miranda, Mr McNumpty and Imamu (wearing a headscarf in case anyone spotted her. People's eyes were still peeled in the area. The 'wild creature' that featured on the news had never been seen since. Well, of course not – it was Imamu). They all piled into the little blue Honda.

Imamu wasn't happy about the headscarf. 'Do I have to wear

this ridiculous thing? It's very itchy and I can't hear properly.'

'I think it rather suits you,' winked Uncle Tony.

'Don't worry, Mum. Mrs Dobson doesn't live far away.'

'Good,' said Uncle Tony. 'It's a bit squashed in the back here!'

'Me squashy too!' said Miranda, sounding even more high-pitched than usual.

Ten minutes later the Honda pulled up outside a pleasant terraced house in Hampton Wick. Everyone climbed out and headed for the front door. There was a small, neat front garden, and thick net curtains covered all of the windows. Mr Bold rang the bell.

There was the sound of the front door being unlocked and then the rattle of a chain being removed. Finally the door opened and the smiling face of Mrs Dobson appeared.

'Ah, I thought it was you, Mr Bold!' she said. 'Do come in, all of you.'

In the lounge the coffee table was heaving with freshly made cakes and sandwiches, glasses of lemonade and teacups. Imamu immediately tore off the annoying headscarf and scoffed a couple of cakes.

'Grandma, wait!' laughed Betty. 'Humans like to offer you a cake – you don't just help yourself!'

'Really?' asked Imamu. 'I'll never understand humans!'

'You'd better explain to Mrs Dobson about your mother, Fred.'

'Ah, yes. Our happy hyena family has had a visitor: my mother has come to stay with us from Africa. Mum, this is Mrs Dobson.'

Mrs Dobson hesitantly patted Imamu on the head. 'Er, pleased to meet you,' she said. 'Was your mother the wild beast on the loose that I read about in the papers, Mr Bold?'

'Yes!' laughed Fred. 'My mother is very much a wild hyena. Hence the lack of table manners.'

'She's not going to make a mess on my clean carpet,

is she?' said Mrs Dobson, looking worried.

'I'm on my best behaviour,' said Imamu. 'Don't worry.'

'Please, do have some more cakes,' offered Mrs Dobson.

Imamu didn't wait to be asked twice. She reached forward and scooped up a vanilla slice with her big, pink tongue.

'I like a woman with a good appetite,' remarked Uncle Tony.

'Thank you so much for coming, everyone,' said Mrs Dobson. 'It is really *so* good of you to offer to help. My poor son . . .' And she began to dab her eyes with a handkerchief.

'Where is he?' asked Mrs Bold.

'Upstairs. He doesn't come out of his room. Not unless there is a wildlife programme on the television. Especially if there are monkeys or chimps on. That is what he wants to be. Always has, ever since he was little. My husband always said it was a phase he'd grow out of, but he never has. He's got more chimp-like as the years have gone by. My husband is rather embarrassed by him. I just want to help him, though. Get him out of his room and start living his life.'

'Does he get lonely up there?' asked Mr McNumpty.

Mrs Dobson nodded. 'Yes, he does.'

'He no happy?' asked Miranda.

'No. He hasn't been for a long time. I just want him to be himself and be happy.'

Miranda looked around, as if someone might overhear her. 'Me monkey,' she whispered. 'Me teach him monkey A-B-C!'

'Oh my goodness!' said Mrs Dobson, almost dropping her tea. 'You're a monkey? I thought you were a hairy toddler. Jeffrey will be so excited to meet you! All of you!'

'And we want to do all we can to help you both, Mrs Dobson,' said Mrs Bold.

'Please, call me Margaret,' Mrs Dobson reminded them. 'Shall I go and get him?'

A moment later everyone sat in silence listening to the gentle, coaxing voice of Margaret upstairs, then the sound of footsteps on the stairs.

Finally the living-room doors opened again.

'Here we are, Jeffrey. Some real African animals have come to see you,' said Mrs Dobson as she entered the lounge. Following her in cautiously, and clinging to her hand, was a very hairy young man. 'This is Jeffrey, everyone,' said Mrs Dobson as the young man squatted in front of the visitors and stared at them.

Jeffrey had tousled black hair falling over his eyes and down his neck. His long arms and

legs were also quite hairy and he nervously scratched his chest, grunting gently. Mrs Dobson scratched his back reassuringly.

'Jeffrey, meet the Bolds.'

Jeffrey's kind eyes looked around at everyone. He gave a low hoot.

Miranda replied with a similar noise, and jumped down from Uncle Tony's shoulder to sit before the monkey man.

'Hok, hok, ooo, ooo!' said Miranda.

'Hok, hok!' replied Jeffrey, his eyes shining with recognition.

'I wonder what that means?' asked Mr McNumpty, his voice full of wonder.

'Warning call. Aerial threat, possibly an eagle,' replied Jeffrey.

'Yes!' said Miranda. 'You speaky good chimp already!'

'Of course I do!' said Jeffrey. 'I've been learning for years but I've had no one to speak it with.'

The ice was broken, and to Mrs Dobson's delight all the animals gathered around her son, sniffing him ('Nice . . . quite chimp-like, but a bit of a hint of soap there'), examining his hair ('Bit too long, unless you're going for the orang-utan look, in which case you need to dye it red. Roots could be a problem. Advise against') and teeth ('Need to be sharper. Could we file them down?').

'So you're not living full-time as a chimp?' asked Mr McNumpty, once the examination was over.

'No. But I'd like to,' replied Jeffrey, now sitting cross-legged on the sofa, nibbling on a cucumber sandwich. 'I've known I was a monkey for as long as I can remember. I am a chimpanzee trapped in a human body.'

'What would make you happy, young chap?'

200

asked Mr McNumpty.

'To live in Africa and be a chimp full-time.'

Mrs Dobson dabbed at her eyes with a handkerchief again.

'Oh, Margaret,' said Mrs Bold. 'This must be so hard for you.'

Margaret nodded. 'Yes. But what is harder? Knowing you won't see your son any more or knowing he is unhappy?'

'You could still see me, Mum,' said Jeffrey. 'Africa isn't on the Moon, you know.'

'That is true,' said Mrs Dobson, forcing a smile. 'But Jeffrey, are you *sure* this is what you want? Living in Africa as a chimpanzee? It's a huge decision.'

'I've never been more sure of anything, Mum. There is no doubt in my mind. I'm just not sure how I am going to achieve it. Staying in my room upstairs, perched on top of the wardrobe eating bananas and making chimp noises isn't going to satisfy me for much longer. I need to go to the next stage.'

Mr Bold decided to lighten the mood with some monkey jokes:

Where do chimps get their gossip from?

The ape vine!

'Yes, thank you, Fred. Very funny. But how are we going to help Jeffrey?' asked Mrs Bold.

'I'll take him back to Africa with *me*,' said Imamu. 'Once I work out a way to get home, that is.'

'But will he be accepted by the other chimps?' asked Mrs Dobson fearfully. 'Is he convincing enough?'

'Not really, no,' said Imamu rather brutally. 'I'd know he wasn't a real chimp right away.'

Jeffrey looked a little offended. 'Then what's the point?' he said. 'I might as well go back up to my room and live there in my pretend world.'

'No. We can help you!' piped up Betty. 'We've helped lots of animals act human. We can just do it the other way round and help you be more chimp-like. Can't we, Mum? Dad?'

'Of course,' said Mrs Bold reassuringly, hugging her twins affectionately. 'Helping is what we Bolds enjoy.'

'When Imamu is convinced you're a chimp, so will all the wild animals of Africa be! It's just going to take some practice,' said Mr Bold.

'We teachy Jeffrey!' cried Miranda.

'Exactly!' said Mr Bold excitedly. 'I think if Jeffrey came to stay with *us* for a while, we could train him, teach him, transform him into the chimpanzee that he already feels he is. We've done it the other way round – from animal to human – so why not from human to animal?'

'But then what?' asked Jeffrey. 'This is all very kind, but once I am a proper chimp in every respect, how do I get to Africa?'

'Well,' said Fred, 'I'm not sure yet. But you will. We'll find a way.'

'I'm headed back in that direction, as it happens,' offered Imamu. 'I haven't worked out the details yet, but I'm a very determined hyena.'

'She certainly is,' agreed Mrs Bold.

Chapter

The next day a slightly tearful Mrs Dobson delivered Jeffrey to 41 Fairfield Road. He was wearing 'human' clothes to travel in – a light raincoat and a grey beret – and carried a suitcase.

'I brought my ropes with me,' said Jeffrey.

'He likes to *swing* about,' explained Mrs Dobson, handing over a Tupperware box. 'His favourite food. Papaya, watermelon, walnuts and some bananas,' she said.

'Come in and have a cup of tea, Margaret,' said Mrs Bold, putting her arm around the headteacher. 'You're not to worry about Jeffrey. We will take very good care of him. Miranda is looking forward to having another monkey to play with!'

In the kitchen Miranda was perched on top of the fridge, jumping up and down with excitement.

'Me teachy Jeffrey! Me make him very good chimpy!'

Jeffrey's training room was to be the dining room – still an awful mess after Imamu's digging. But actually, the smell of earth and the bits of wood made it a little bit more like somewhere chimps might live; everything really does happen for a reason (as I might have already mentioned).

Mr McNumpty came round from next door with his ladder and helped Mr Bold to tie up the ropes – criss-crossing them from one end of the ceiling to the other, while Jeffrey took his 'human' clothes off in the bathroom and reappeared wearing a tatty loincloth. His mannerisms and appearance were already remarkably ape-like, everyone agreed.

Jeffrey and Miranda began swinging on the ropes, shrieking and enjoying themselves enormously. After a while they stopped for a grooming session, using their fingers to comb through each other's hair and pull out any foreign bodies they came across.

Mrs Bold and Mrs Dobson watched their antics for a while and then closed the door and went into the kitchen to drink their tea.

'He does seem very at home here already,' said Margaret, taking a sip.

'Well, he can socialise with his own kind, can't he? He must have been **very** lonely. Tell me, Margaret, when did it all start?'

'Many years ago,' said Mrs Dobson. 'As a child he could climb trees before he could walk. And when he cried as a baby, it wasn't a normal baby noise at all. I should have guessed then, but of course you don't think – do you? – that your little boy is different in that way.'

'No,' agreed Amelia. 'But all we want, as parents, is for our children to be happy. By bringing him here you have taken the first step towards your son's happiness.'

'I often wonder if it was something I did. Something I said that made him this way.'

'Of course not. He was just born that way. And we have to accept him for who he is.'

'It's just so unusual,' said Mrs Dobson.

'Is it, though, Margaret? There have been sightings of man-monkeys in all parts of the world for centuries. Ape-like men – Bigfoot, the Yeti, the Yowie in Australia, the Big Grey Man of Ben Macdui in Scotland. Others in Sumatra, China, Siberia.'

'Really? So there is nothing strange about my son?'

'Not in my opinion, no,' said Amelia firmly. 'After some time with us I promise you your son will be ready to go and live happily in the wild. He's not the first and he won't be the last.'

'Oh, thank you, Amelia,' said Mrs Dobson, smiling for the first time and finishing the last of her tea. 'You've made me feel *so* much better.'

They both stopped to listen to the happy grunting and whooping noises coming from the next room.

'I'll go now, and let Jeffrey get on with his training.'

Mrs Bold stood up and gave Mrs Dobson a hug. 'And

thank you. A less understanding headteacher might have reported the fact that hyenas were attending her school.'

'Oh, I'd almost forgotten about that!' laughed Mrs Dobson. 'If only humans were as wonderfully kind and helpful as you hyenas, life would be a lot easier. Goodbye, Amelia. I will call in next week, if I may, and see how Jeffrey is getting on.'

'Whenever you like, Margaret. And you're not to worry about a thing.'

'Look after my boy!'

'We will.'

Before she left, Mrs Dobson poked her head round the dining-room door. Miranda and Jeffrey were swinging wildly from the ropes,

215

round and round the room. '*Ooh, oooh, ah, ah, aaah!*'

Margaret smiled to herself as she drove home. Through a remarkable series of events she had found a way to give her beloved son the chance to fulfil his dream.

Chapter

17

The next few weeks were very busy at the Bolds' house, which was just the way they liked it.

Imamu was fully occupied watching the 'monkey's' behaviour and advising Jeffrey when a look or gesture was more human than ape. Every now and then she and Uncle Tony would mount a hyena 'attack' – creeping up on Jeffrey, testing his reactions and ability to leap to safety.

'Too slow! Jump higher! Open your mouth

wider when you screech! Lower your jaw!'
Imamu advised.

'Bare your teeth more!' suggested
Uncle Tony.

Over the following weeks
Jeffrey's arm muscles
strengthened from all the rope-
swinging, and his hair and beard
became more ragged and matted,
covering his human features. Miranda
taught him ape sounds and characteristics.
She taught him how to eat his food in a monkey-
like way and how to wee on the floor – not in
the toilet. (Mrs Bold wasn't too pleased with
that, but agreed it was important, so went to
the pet shop and bought some sawdust.)

Every day after school, Bobby and Betty
went into the dining room with a selection

of fruit that they threw randomly into the air. Jeffrey had to leap around, catching the fruit, flying through the air, sometimes doing somersaults, sharpening his reactions and reflexes, becoming more acrobatic by the day. And each evening he made a sling-bed out of some towels and slept there.

Mr McNumpty did an hour of extensive toe-stretching classes on Jeffrey in the afternoons. He used his strong bear paws to pull Jeffrey's toes in every direction in an attempt to make them more thumb-like – and a little bit longer and more ape-ish.

Every few days the twins' best friend Minnie came to tea and looked in on Jeffrey to see the progress.

'Better every time I look!' she said encouragingly.

But Imamu *still* wasn't convinced. 'Better, definitely, but he's not there yet. Keep practising, young man,' she would say, and then return to the game of dominoes she was playing with Uncle Tony.

After a month it was generally thought that the dining room was too small a space for Jeffrey's training. He needed to get outside and swing from real trees, but how could this be done without attracting unwanted attention or alarm?

'Why don't you go to the New Forest!' suggested Minnie. 'I went there with my parents last year – loads of space and trees. And not many people about.'

'Sounds perfect!' said Mrs Bold.

So the next weekend everyone piled into the Honda and off they went to Hampshire. The drive there was an opportunity for some tree jokes, of course.

What did the little tree say to the big tree?

"Leaf me alone!"

What did the beaver say to the tree?

"It's been nice gnawing you!"

What type of tree fits in your hand?

A palm tree!

They drove to Lymington first, where they stopped to eat their sandwiches, then drove deep into the forest, away from all the tourists. Off the beaten track they ventured, then in amongst the trees where there was no path at all. The light faded as the trees grew thicker and taller, squirrels and birds staring at them as if they had never seen a car before. Eventually, when they were sure no one else was around, Mr Bold parked the car and everyone jumped out. The only sound was the breeze in the trees.

'This is a good spot!' said Mrs Bold. 'We'll stay here on lookout while Miranda and Jeffrey go and have some fun up in the trees.'

'Ooh! Me likey big trees!' said Miranda, gazing up in wonder at the canopy of ancient oak trees, shafts of golden, glittering sunshine breaking through like magical searchlights. 'You ready, Jeffrey?'

Jeffrey nodded and clapped his big hands together before the pair jumped on a low-hanging branch, then slowly leaped and swung from one branch to the next, from this tree to that, higher and higher, until they were so far up in the trees they were just distant, hairy shadows.

The twins, meanwhile, enjoyed running around the forest floor, kicking up the dried leaves and stamping on twigs. Imamu immediately began to forage about. From the noisy crunching sound she made, she had found some tasty snails to eat. Uncle Tony found a sunny glade to take a snooze in. As for Mr McNumpty: well, what do bears normally do in the woods? Of course! He wandered off for a private moment to relieve himself in amongst the ferns.

Everyone was very happy. Mr and Mrs Bold

could hear the distant whoops of joy from Miranda and Jeffrey, high above them and far away.

Then suddenly Mrs Bold's ears detected something different in their calls.

'Fred?' she said, cocking her ear to one side. 'Listen. Something sounds wrong. Can you hear?'

Mr Bold turned his head this way and that, listening intently. 'Yes,' he said. 'That is a chimp's warning call, I believe.'

Far away, mingled with the breeze, came the urgent sound: 'Hok! Hok! Woo! Ooo!'

'Definitely,' agreed Mrs Bold. 'Whatever can it be?'

'And there is another sound too,' said Mr Bold. 'Coming from the other direction.'

Mrs Bold stood up and sniffed the air. 'I hear it, Fred,' she said. 'It is the sound of an engine. Coming this way!'

'I think Miranda and Jeffrey are warning us about something.'

'Quick, get your mother in the car. Whoever it is doesn't want to meet a wild naked hyena in the middle of the woods. It will frighten the life out of them,' said Mrs Bold urgently. 'Bobby! Betty! Come and get in the car please!'

Mr Bold immediately called his mother (in hyena): several loud barks and a shrill howl.

Imamu knew this meant **danger** and she instantly ran to Fred. 'What is it, Spot?' she asked.

'In the boot, Mum. Can't explain now.'

Imamu could tell from her son's tone that this was no time to shilly-shally. She jumped into the boot and Fred threw a blanket over her.

The rumble of a car engine was getting closer . . .

Chapter

The Bolds looked at each other in alarm. Yes, the car was certainly heading their way.

'I'll go and wake up Uncle Tony. He's too deaf to hear us calling him,' said Mrs Bold, heading quickly for the sunny spot from where the gentle snoring of an elderly hyena was coming.

She shook Uncle Tony awake.

'Something is happening. Not sure what. You'd better wake up and get in the car, Uncle Tony!'

Half asleep, the old boy needed help from Mrs Bold to stand up. She walked him quickly to the car, where he joined a worried-looking Betty and Bobby on the back seat.

By now the approaching car was just a few hundred metres away, weaving through the trees, headlights on. It was some kind of jeep, guessed Mr Bold.

'Where is Mr McNumpty?' asked Mrs Bold.

'He wandered off to do his business. I don't know in which direction.'

'Oh no!' said a worried Amelia.

The jeep then arrived and a man and a woman got out: forest wardens, wearing official uniforms and looking rather cross.

'Hey!' shouted the woman sternly. 'What are you doing in this part of the forest?'

'Oh, hello there!' said Mr Bold, with his widest smile. 'Us? Here? Oh yes, so we are!'

'You're in a conservation area,' said the man accusingly. 'Did you not see the signs?'

'Signs? Why, no, we saw no signs,' said Mr Bold. 'Did you see any signs, Mrs Bold?'

'I saw no sign of a sign,' replied Amelia.

'We definitely didn't see any signs at all,' confirmed Mr Bold.

'Well, you shouldn't be here,' said the first warden.

'No, we definitely shouldn't,' said Mr Bold,

thinking it was always best to agree with authority figures. 'I blame the car,' he said, giving the Honda a light slap. 'Naughty, naughty car!'

'Why is it the car's fault?' asked the warden.

'Very lazy,' said Mr Bold, shaking his head.

'A lazy car?' asked the man, scratching his head.

'Oh yes,' continued Mr Bold. 'It's the wheels. Always tired.'

'Tired?'

'Tyred! Do you get it? Tired wheels!'

Mrs Bold giggled – 'Oh, very good, Fred!' – but the wardens didn't.

What do you get when dinosaurs crash their cars?

Tyrannosaurus wrecks!

The twins and Uncle Tony giggled from inside the car. Bobby wound down the windows so as not to miss the next joke.

What do you get when you cross a fly, a car and a dog?

A flying car-pet!

Mrs Bold, Bobby, Betty and Uncle Tony laughed heartily. The blanket covering Imamu vibrated too.

'More, more!' cried the twins.

'Now, listen,' said the warden, his hands on his hips. 'We are very busy. I haven't got time to listen to all this nonsense. I'm here to tell you off! You're trespassing.'

Mr Bold thought for a moment. Jokes were usually the answer to any predicament, so he pressed on and tried another.

Why was the woman fired from the car assembly line?

Because she was caught taking a brake!

But the wardens were stony-faced. One more, Fred thought.

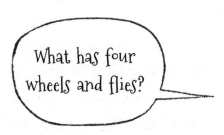

What has four wheels and flies?

Then before he could give the answer, the female warden jumped in:

A rubbish truck!

'Wow, you knew that one?' said Mr Bold, impressed.

'A lucky guess,' said the warden, smiling modestly.

But her partner tapped his foot impatiently. 'Ahem!' He cleared his throat. 'You and your family should not be in this part of the forest, do you understand? This is for wildlife only. You're disturbing the animals.'

There was a muffled bark from under the blanket.

'What was that?' asked the warden suspiciously.

'Oh, excuse me,' said Uncle Tony, patting his stomach. 'Bit of indigestion.'

'You must leave straightaway,' continued the warden, taking out a notebook and pen and writing down the registration number of the blue Honda.

'Oh, but we can't leave,' said Mrs Bold, sounding alarmed and looking up into the trees. 'Not yet.'

'Excuse me?' said the warden.

'Er, my wife means that our neighbour, Mr McNumpty, has just gone to answer a call of nature,' explained Fred. 'He won't be long.'

'Well, where is he?' asked the warden.

'Er,' said Fred vaguely, 'he's a very private man. In fact, that is why we drove so far into the forest, so he could find somewhere quiet to, er, perform, as it were. He can't bear anyone around while he is, er, dropping the kids off at the pool, if you know what I mean. I'm sure you understand?'

'Not really, no.'

'You run along and we will be off just as soon as he's done. Terribly sorry for the misunderstanding. We'll stay on the roads in future. Good day to you.'

But Fred's attempts to get rid of the wardens weren't working.

'There is a problem in this area with poachers, Mr . . . ?'

'Bold, Fred Bold. This is my lovely wife, Amelia, and our two mischievous twins, Bobby and Betty there in the car with dear Uncle Tony. Not as young as he used to be, but he still has all his own teeth. Do you? I—'

'Mr Bold,' interrupted the male warden, getting exasperated with Fred's time-wasting.

'You and your family do not seem to fit the *usual* description of poachers, but nevertheless I'd be failing in my duty if I didn't see you out of these woods before I went on my way. If that's all right with you?'

'Er, of course, Mr Warden. Quite right too.'

There was an awkward pause during which the warden looked at his watch and raised his eyebrows. 'So. Where is your **mysterious** friend, Mr Bold? Does he usually take this long in the . . . bathroom?'

'Er,' said Mr Bold.

Just then there was a rustling from the clump of ferns a few metres away and there was Mr McNumpty lumbering somewhat awkwardly towards them, his big coat buttoned up to the collar.

'Yoo-hoo!' he said. 'That's a lot better. Sorry to keep you. Last night's brown rice and aubergine bake just working its way through.' He rubbed his tummy. 'Oh, I see we have visitors?'

'Nigel, these are the New Forest wardens. We shouldn't be here. They want us to leave,' said Mr Bold.

'Right-o,' said Mr McNumpty, who seemed to have got wider than before . . . 'I'll squeeze into the car then, shall I, and we'll be off.'

He winked at Mrs Bold and tapped the side of his nose. 'Don't mind if I take the front seat, do you?'

'But what about Mir—' began Betty, but her sentence was interrupted by Mrs Bold.

'Shift up in the back, children,' she said brightly. 'Fred? Start the car.'

'Stay on the roads in future, please,' said the male warden sternly.

'We will do, many apologies. Very silly of us!' said Mrs Bold.

As Mr McNumpty lowered himself into the front seat there was a squeak from inside his coat and an '00f!' sound from somewhere around his nether regions.

'Aaah! Tally-ho!' said Mr McNumpty loudly. 'I really must go on a diet sometime, really I must!'

'Sorry for the misunderstanding, Mr and Ms Warden,' said Mr Bold, putting the car into first gear and slowly driving off through the trees in the direction of the track. The wardens got into their jeep and followed the Bolds' Honda, each keeping a close eye on the strange family in the blue car ahead.

'But – Miranda and Jeffrey!' said a worried Bobby in a loud whisper. 'We can't leave them behind!'

'Don't worry, I don't think we have,' said Mrs Bold, pointing discreetly at Mr McNumpty sitting in front of her.

Then Mr McNumpty undid the top button

of his coat and put his snout inside. 'Hold on, chaps,' he said. 'Not much longer.' A strangled cry and a breathless groan seemed to come from somewhere inside his coat, which seemed to be moving about in a very unusual way.

'Oh no – has he swallowed them?' asked Betty.

'I hope not. We'll find out in a minute,' said her mother.

A few moments later they were out of the woods and on the main track. Shortly after, the warden's jeep tooted them and the wardens raised their hands in a half-wave, half-salute.

'Byeee!' called Mr Bold.

'Hurry uppy!' came a cry from inside Mr McNumpty's coat, then there was a ripping sound and a large, hairy leg emerged from his shoulder.

'Ooh-argh! I've got cramp! Help!'

'That's Jeffrey!' said Betty. 'However did he hide himself in Mr McNumpty's coat?'

'Pull over and I'll show you,' said Nigel. By now the lower leg of the chimp man had wound itself around the back of his thick grizzly bear neck, the foot waving with distress.

Mr Bold checked in his rear-view mirror to see that the wardens' jeep was out of sight. It was, so he pulled over and jumped out of the car and ran round to the passenger seat. 'Let's get you out, quickly!' he said.

Mr McNumpty got his legs out of the car, but was struggling to lower his head out of the door frame. 'Oops – can you pull me please, Fred? I'm stuck!' he said, sounding desperate. 'Soon as you can . . .'

'I'll help,' said Amelia, jumping out of the back seat. Bobby and Betty, you push from inside.'

In the end it took all of the Bolds several minutes to get the enlarged Mr McNumpty out of the Honda. By then, two legs and a monkey's head had appeared through various rips in his coat.

'Oh, at last,' Mr McNumpty said, finally standing on the grass verge. He let out a massive sigh of relief, then quickly unbuttoned his coat and dropped it to the ground, revealing the two stowaways. Jeffrey was upside down, panting for breath, his head between his host's legs. His strong arms were clinging to Mr McNumpty's waist, his knees over Nigel's shoulders and his body flattened against Nigel's back. Miranda, looking hot and squashed, had her little arms round his tummy, the rest of her squeezed in between Jeffrey's legs. She leaped to freedom straight away and lay on the grass, breathing in the lovely fresh air.

'Poor Miranda looks cross-eyed!' said Mrs Bold, giving the poor animal a gentle pat on her back. Miranda looked thankful, then bounded over to her favourite place – on Uncle Tony's shoulder.

'Me very hotty and bothery!' she squeaked.

Free at last, Jeffrey did a sort of somersault, landing on his feet. He wiggled his cramped feet and grinned happily at everyone. 'Phew!' was all he said between breaths. 'Phew! Phew! Phew!'

'How clever of you, Nigel,' said Mrs Bold. 'I didn't know what we were going to do. The wardens were insisting we leave the woods, and as far as I knew, poor Miranda and Jeffrey were high up in the trees. We almost had to abandon them!'

Mr McNumpty was busy adjusting his tie. 'Fear not. I heard those pesky wardens' car while I was, er, making myself comfortable in the ferns.'

'And we see Mister MickyNumptee from tree toppy!' joined in Miranda.

'I could smell trouble,' continued Mr McNumpty.

'Not surprised, given what *you* were up to,' said Fred.

'No! I don't mean poo, Fred. Really!' said

Nigel indignantly. 'I mean, trouble for Miranda and Jeffrey. Our experiment – to let them be real apes in real trees was in grave danger of going very **very** wrong. So I whistled. We signalled to each other. Hand signals – or paw signals if you prefer. While you were telling your jokes to the wardens I concealed them about my person. Not easy. Not for any of us. But, hey ho, here we are! Still in one piece – apart from my coat – and still all together!'

'Hurrah! I don't know what I'd have done without my Miranda,' said Uncle Tony. 'Three cheers for Mr McNumpty!'

But the cheers were interrupted by an angry banging sound coming from the boot of the car.

'Oh, Mum!' cried Fred, rushing back to the Honda and opening the boot.

Imamu leaped out, looking furious. 'Fancy forgetting about *me*!' she said.

'Sorry, Mum. There was a bit of an emergency.'

'So I understand,' snapped Imamu. 'I look forward to hearing what sort of emergency means you have to shove your own mother under a smelly old blanket and lock her inside a cramped car boot! I've a good mind to—' But her tirade was interrupted when she caught sight of something out the corner of her eye. A squirrel was peering at the strange gathering from a branch of a tree a few metres away. Within five seconds Imamu had, with lightning speed, run, caught and eaten it.

'There,' she said, spitting out a bit of squirrel tail. 'That has put me in a better mood. This day out has suddenly improved!'

'We're not allowed to do that,' said Betty, feeling a little jealous.

'Shame,' said Imamu. 'That's because you live like humans, I expect. Not many humans go around eating squirrels. But I, should you need reminding, am a wild hyena. I eat squirrels. So there. And if there was a deer about I'd eat that too.' She looked around hungrily.

'Let's all get back in the car and go home,' said Fred a little agitatedly. 'Before the wardens come to see what we're up to again.'

Chapter

So the outing to the New Forest was not without incident. But by the time everyone got back to Fairfield Road, Mr Bold had managed to put a positive spin on things.

'Well, it proves *one* thing,' he said. 'Jeffrey is as capable as any chimpanzee. I saw how he swung through the treetops! Masterful!'

'And he spotty danger!' said Miranda. 'Just like monkey. And he warned the rest of us.'

'So is he ready to go to Africa and start his new life?' questioned Mrs Bold.

Jeffrey (who had given up speaking human altogether these days) jumped up and down excitedly.

'Jeffrey say yes,' said Miranda.

'What do you think, Mother?' Mr Bold asked Imamu. 'Could he pass for a chimp in the wild?'

'I never thought it possible,' replied Imamu. 'But I actually think he could. And, let's face it, if *you* can pass for a human then I'm pretty sure he can pass for a chimp.'

Jeffrey threw his big chimp arms around himself and beat happily on his chest.

'Hmmm . . .' said Uncle Tony. 'But there's only one problem. How do we get him there?'

'And me,' muttered Imamu. 'I can't hack it here for much longer. Love you all, but I need to get home.'

'So the question is,' summarised Mr McNumpty, 'how we are going to transport a wild hyena and a man who thinks and lives convincingly as a chimp, to Africa. We need to think about the details now.'

A contemplative silence descended over the Bolds' lounge.

'Could we send them in a parcel?' offered Betty.

'Er, no, dear,' said Mrs Bold. 'It would take too long and they might get thirsty.'

'Can't Mr McNumpty hide Jeffrey under his coat like he did in the New Forest?' suggested Bobby.

'That was just for five minutes!' protested Mr McNumpty. 'Neither of us could manage hours on a plane. And besides, he'd show up on those X-ray machines.'

'Oh,' said Bobby despondently.

'I wonder if your friend at the airport might help you again?' asked Mrs Bold of Imamu.

'Dolores? She would help if she could. But she doesn't have contacts in England.'

'Yes. Point taken,' said Amelia.

A little while later Mrs Dobson popped round for her weekly update on Jeffrey's progress. She sat scratching her son's chin, while Bobby and Betty told her all about their adventure in the New Forest and the unexpected interruption from the wardens.

'What a clever chimp you are!' she said when she heard how Jeffrey had hid under Mr McNumpty's big coat.

'So now we think Jeffrey is ready, Mrs Dobson,' said Mr Bold.

'Ready for his new life in Africa? Would you like that, Jeffrey?'

Jeffrey made it clear that he would, honking loudly and nodding.

'I think so too,' said Mrs Dobson. 'I can hardly remember you as you once were. Remarkable!'

'But now we have to find a way to get Jeffrey – and Imamu – to Africa.'

'Well, I was thinking about that,' said Mrs Dobson.

'Oh yes?' said Mrs Bold.

'Yes. I was thinking I might like to go too.'

'You want to live as a wild chimp woman?' gasped Betty.

'No, dear,' laughed Mrs Dobson. 'But I've been doing some research. There are no chimps in the Serengeti. The Gombe National Park in Tanzania is where wild chimps live. School summer holidays are coming up. I was thinking I could go on holiday. Fly over for a few weeks. That way I could go for a walk in the jungle every day and give Jeffrey a wave. See that he was all right. Maybe throw him a few bananas.'

'Excellent idea!' said Mr Bold. And as Jeffrey was now lying on his back having his tummy rubbed, with a big smile on his face, he clearly agreed too.

'But how does that help us get Jeffrey to Africa?' asked Uncle Tony.

'He has a passport,' said Mrs Dobson simply. She lowered her voice so as not to offend her son. 'He wasn't *born* a chimp, was he? Somewhere under there is also a human!'

'Of course!' said Mrs Bold. 'How silly of me to have forgotten. But to travel there on the plane, Jeffrey would have to go back to being human again. Just for the day. Do you think he can remember what to do?'

Everyone looked doubtfully at Jeffrey, who was now picking at his feet with his long, dirty nails, not listening to them at all.

'Oh dear,' said Mrs Dobson. 'How very confusing for him. And after all your hard work chimpy-fying him!'

'A means to an end, that's all!' said

Mr McNumpty. 'Leave it to me. Oi, Jeffrey!'
he said sharply.

Jeffrey looked up from his task.

'Want to go to Tanzania and live with the
wild chimps?'

Jeffrey's eyes filled with tears of joy and he
nodded enthusiastically.

'Good. And would you do absolutely anything to be able to go to Africa?'

Jeffrey nodded some more.

'Anything at all?'

More nodding.

'Now, I know you don't want to be a human. You probably don't even consider yourself a human any more, do you?'

Jeffrey shook his head vehemently.

'No. And you're not. You're a chimp-man! But listen to me, old chap. To get you to Africa, you're going to have to be a human one last time.'

Jeffrey looked alarmed.

'Just for one day. One tiny, little day. Worth it, though. A means to an end. Then as soon as you get there – off you go. Free at last. You understand?'

Jeffrey nodded sadly, then went back to picking his feet.

'There we are! Job done!' said Mr McNumpty.

Imamu cleared her throat. 'And what about me?' she demanded. 'How am *I* going to get home to the Serengeti?'

But no one had an answer just yet.

Chapter

The next day Mrs Dobson booked two flights to Tanzania and a holiday for one at a safari camp in Tanzania. She and Jeffrey would be leaving in just three weeks' time. Jeffrey's lessons continued but, rather confusingly, he then had to spend a few hours each afternoon relearning how to be a human, so that he could use a toilet, take a shower and eat his food with cutlery on the journey, arousing no suspicion. Multi-tasking. It was difficult: the more ape-like he became, the trickier it was to walk and talk like a human. But it would all be worth it in the end, as everyone kept telling him.

'No painy no gainy!' Miranda said.

But what about Imamu? Was she to be trapped in England for ever? She didn't want to spend the rest of her life washing dishes with her tongue and learning to play dominoes and chess with Uncle Tony – fond as she was of him. No, she wanted to run free on the Serengeti plains, chasing antelope, cackling loudly and scavenging like a proper hyena.

The solution to Imamu's predicament came one morning following an urgent tapping on the window.

'I remember that sound!' said Mrs Bold. 'It's Hector, I'm sure of it!'

And indeed it was. Mrs Bold opened the window and the cuckoo bird flew into the lounge and settled himself on top of the

television. Everyone gathered round to greet their old friend.

'Great to see you again!' said Uncle Tony.

'And look, my mother arrived, just as you said she would!' exclaimed Fred.

Imamu wagged her tail. 'Ah, Hector, my old mate!'

Hector was delighted to see the hyena he had last chatted to thousands of miles away in Africa.

'Wow, you made it over for your visit then?'

'Yup!' said Imamu. 'Once a hyena decides to do something, nothing will stand in their way.'

'And are you enjoying your time here?'

'Loving seeing my family.' Imamu looked affectionately around the room. 'Their new life is something I could never have imagined . . . but I'm ready to go back to Africa now – if I can only think of a way to get there.'

'Shall I see if I can find you some caterpillars?' Bobby offered Hector.

'Oh, that would be most welcome,' said Hector, balancing on one leg and almost toppling over. Bobby ran out to the vegetable patch.

'Hector, what happened to your leg?' asked Mrs Bold, concerned. The bird sighed and shook his head.

'Awful business,' he said. 'I was having a

quiet drink by a pond in Twickenham. There was some fishing wire and I got caught up in it. Stuck for days, I was. Finally I got free, but my leg is taking a long time to heal up.'

'Oh, you poor little thing!' said Mrs Bold.

'I don't like to make a fuss.'

Just then Bobby returned with a saucer full of caterpillars and Hector's eyes brightened up considerably.

'Delicious!' he said, eating them quickly one after the other. 'My injured leg has affected my balance somewhat. I'm not as fast as I was, so catching bugs has become a bit tricky. They're often too quick for me!'

'A wounded animal or bird is easy prey, we find in the wild,' said Imamu a tad insensitively.

'Er, yes, I know,' said Hector. 'So I have made a decision. I'm not **strong** enough to fly to Africa this year. We cuckoos need to fatten ourselves up for the journey and I'm not sure I'd make it, to be honest.'

'But won't a British winter be too cold for you?' asked Betty.

'You can come and live here with us, Hector,' invited Mr Bold. 'We have central heating! You'll be nice and warm.'

'Very kind of you,' said Hector. 'But I *am* going back to Africa. It's just that I'm not going to fly there.'

'Really? Then how are you getting there?' asked Mr McNumpty, frowning.

'By boat,' stated Hector. 'Setting sail tomorrow from Southampton. I've come to say goodbye.'

'A boat sailing all the way from here to Africa?' asked Imamu, her ears pricking up.

'Well, yacht, really,' corrected Hector. 'A luxury yacht, in fact.'

'Tell me more,' said Imamu, moving closer to the cuckoo and listening intently.

'You've heard of the supermodel Gi-Gi?'

Everyone gasped.

'Oh, of course,' said Mr McNumpty. 'Famous for her extraordinarily long neck and fabulous cheekbones.'

'Recently married an uber-rich Russian property magnate?'

'That's the one,' nodded Hector. 'Well, Gi-Gi is, in fact, a giraffe!'

'Always had my suspicions!' said Betty.

'And they are sailing to Cape Town for a belated honeymoon,' continued Hector. 'I had a discreet word with her when she wafted onto her balcony at Claridge's the other day after a photoshoot. I told her about my predicament. She is happy for me to hitch a lift. I'm having my own cabin, in fact! Such a kind giraffe, er, I mean woman. Whatever she is. Anyway, how lucky am I?'

'Hurrah!' said Bobby.

'Such wonderful news,' said Mrs Bold.

272

Mr Bold jumped in with a joke:

Knock knock!

Who's there?

Eileen!

Eileen who?

Eileen-ed over and fell in the water!

There was so much laughter at Mr Bold's interjection that of course he told another.

> How do you know when a yacht is happy?

> When it hugs the shore!

Imamu by now had begun to **salivate** and was pacing up and down the lounge.

'What's up, Mum?' asked Fred.

'This is my opportunity, don't you see?'

'Opportunity for what? To meet a supermodel?'

Imamu sighed loudly. 'For a hyena you can sometimes be rather **stupid**.' She turned her attention back to Hector. 'Hector, my dear friend. Tell me about this trip you're going on . . .'

'We sail at seven o'clock tomorrow evening. From Southampton to Cape Town. Travelling at an average of ten knots, we should complete the journey in twenty-nine days, by my calculations. Cape Town is a fair distance from the Serengeti, of course. But at least I'll be on the right continent. And I should have built my strength up by then . . . all that caviar! Besides, Gi-Gi said it was very possible she could persuade her husband to sail on a bit to Mozambique . . . just a hop and a skip from home!'

'Perfect!' said Imamu. 'You remember how we helped each other before? You told us where we could get a meal and I let you pick away at my fleas and ticks?'

'Yes, **happy days**!' said Hector.

'Well, how's about I come
with you on this yacht? I
really need to get home. In fact, I've been
a little worried that I'll never work out a
way to get there. This seems too good an
opportunity to miss. Perhaps your wounded
leg happened for a reason. Do you think
Gi-Gi would look kindly on another fellow
animal from Africa joining her?'

'Don't hyenas eat giraffes, given the
opportunity?'

'And hyenas eat cuckoos too. But if it is in
my interests not to eat Gi-Gi – and that would
seem to be the case – then of course I wouldn't
dream of doing such a thing!'

'Well, there will be plenty of room in my

cabin. And it would be nice to have some company,' said Hector. 'I'm sure Gi-Gi won't mind.'

'Sorted, then!' said Imamu excitedly. 'Fred, you'll drive me to Southampton in the Honda tomorrow, won't you?'

'Er, yes, Mum, of course I will,' said Fred, taken by surprise at this sudden turn of events.

'Hector, I'll meet you at Southampton docks at six o'clock tomorrow evening.'

'Right-o.'

'What's the name of Gi-Gi's yacht?'

'It's called *Cecily's Delight*.'

And so it was that the conundrum of Imamu's passage back to Africa was suddenly resolved.

The Bolds quickly arranged a last-night party for Imamu. Mr Bold went to Minnie's dad's butcher's shop and returned with lots of big bones for everyone to gnaw on. (Of course, they drew the curtains first.) Uncle Tony serenaded Imamu with some hyena wailing from the old country, and Mr Bold tried out some of his new jokes.

But by the end of the evening, Mr Bold suddenly noticed that his children were no longer laughing and were looking rather downhearted.

'What's wrong, kids? Not enough bones? Don't worry – there are plenty more in the fridge.'

'No, Dad, it's not that. We're just feeling sad about Grandma leaving. We've loved having her here. We might never see her again.'

Mr Bold put an arm round his children. 'I understand how you're feeling – why, I feel the same myself. Having my mother here has been something I never dared dream about, and I've loved every minute of it. But this isn't the life for her and keeping her here will only make her sad. As Mrs Dobson has taught us, sometimes, if you love someone, you have to let them be free. Even if that really hurts.'

Imamu, sensing there was sadness coming from one side of the room, wandered over. 'What's going on here? You look like humans with your miserable faces,' she said. 'Come on, cheer up. You're hyenas. You should be laughing.'

'The twins are sad that you're going, Mum,' Mr Bold told her.

'Ahh,' said Imamu as she nipped the twins' ears. 'And I shall be very sad to leave you, my darlings. Finding you both has been one of the most wonderful moments of my life and I am so very proud of you both. You are handsome, fast, strong hyenas full of fun and laughter. But on top of that you have human skills I have come to admire. You are polite, you are considerate, you think of others and you use the toilet beautifully. Wait until I tell the family back home about you. They just won't believe it. I know it will be hard for us to see each other again but please remember that where there's a will there's a way, and if ever you tire of your human life and would like to go a bit wild – well, you know where to find me.'

The twins hugged their grandma tightly and Mr Bold wiped a tear from his eye.

Chapter

Less than twenty-four hours later the Bolds were all at Southampton docks.

Earlier that day Mr Bold had gone to the supermarket to get a large, sturdy cardboard box.

After fond farewells, Imamu jumped inside the box and, with Hector fluttering around above them, two tattooed dock workers wearing overalls carried the box up the gangplank of *Cecily's Delight*. The Bolds watched anxiously, but apart from a slight mishap, when the box was nearly dropped over the side into the sea, everything went according to plan. Once the box was onboard and taken safely below deck, Mrs Bold wiped a tear from her eye.

'Safe journey, Imamu!' Uncle Tony said quietly.

'Bon voyage!' said Fred.

The Bolds stood and watched as the crew of *Cecily's Delight* untied ropes and prepared to set sail. Then, just before departure, Hector flew out of an open porthole and landed on the railings of the dock.

'Well, I guess this is it,' he said.

'You *will* look after our grandma for us, won't you?' said Betty.

'I promise,' said Hector sincerely.

'Will she get enough food?' asked Bobby.

'Oh yes, definitely,' replied Hector. 'I've already had a word with Gi-Gi, and extra provisions have been ordered. Especially steak and chops!'

The twins smiled. 'Thank you, Hector.'

'This has all worked out so splendidly for her,' said Uncle Tony.

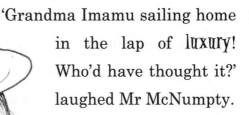

'Grandma Imamu sailing home in the lap of luxury! Who'd have thought it?' laughed Mr McNumpty.

'Imamu is going to teach me to play chess to pass the time on the journey,' said Hector. 'She says you've taught her well, Tony – and it will make a change for me not having to learn facts from the encyclopaedia all the way.'

'Mind she no chewy up chess pieces!' said Miranda.

'If you see her with a bishop in her mouth, tell her off at once!' said Uncle Tony.

'Now I'd better be off,' said Hector. 'Don't worry about a thing. All will be well, I promise. I will be flying back to Teddington next spring, so I'll tell you all the news then.' Hector fluttered up in the air and circled around the Bolds, cuckoo-ing a fond farewell.

'Goodbye, Hector!' said Mr Bold.

'See you next year!' said Mrs Bold.

'Love to Grandma!' called the twins.

Then Hector flew back to the yacht and through the open porthole.

A few minutes later the boat began to move regally out of Southampton dock and proceed gently out to sea.

The Bolds stayed watching and waving until, even with their superior hyena eyesight, they could see her no more.

The next few weeks passed quickly at 41 Fairfield Road. Jeffrey's dual training, both as ape and human, progressed well. He excelled at his ape behaviour, and although he didn't enjoy being a human, he had several outings to the park, escorted by the twins,

Mr McNumpty and Uncle Tony, and he managed to walk along the paths and chat to passers-by convincingly and resist the temptation to scratch his bottom, climb trees or swing from the climbing frame in the children's play area. It seemed that he would be able to go through the airport and travel on the plane without alarming anyone, when the time came.

'I don't like it when people go,' said Bobby, the night before Mrs Dobson and Jeffrey were to leave for Africa. The twins were in bed and Mrs Bold was just tucking them in and giving them both a goodnight kiss.

'I understand that,' said Mrs Bold. 'But it helps to look at things differently sometimes.'

'What do you mean, Mum?' asked Betty.

'Well,' said Amelia, turning on the night light and sitting on the end of Betty's bed. 'Sometimes we focus on what makes *us* happy, but sometimes other people's happiness is more important than what *we* want. Jeffrey has been a part of our family, so he always will be.'

'And now he's going far away and I'll miss him!' said Bobby.

'Me missy Jeffrey too!' said Miranda sadly. She was perched on the windowsill, her little monkey head poking out through the curtains. None of them felt much like sleeping. They were too sad.

'Missing someone means you care about them,' said Mrs Bold. 'But this is Jeffrey's moment – what he has always, always wanted! He is leaving us but starting his new adventure. Close your eyes now, and when you think about missing Jeffrey, just replace those thoughts with a picture of Jeffrey living free and happy in Africa.'

The twins and Miranda closed their eyes. Then, as they did as Mrs Bold suggested, their sad expressions turned to smiles.

'And remember all the others who have joined our family and then moved on. Sheila the crocodile, now swimming down the Nile. How happy she is!

'Roger the sheep, looking after children, working as the most wonderful nanny. How happy he is!

'The two racehorses, Minty Boy and Gangster's Moll, out in the fresh air working as landscape gardeners. How happy they are!

'Fifi Lampadaire the French poodle, living her dream as a singing sensation on a cruise ship. How happy she is!'

As she spoke, Mrs Bold's voice became quieter and quieter until she was almost whispering.

Mr Bold came into the twins' bedroom now, and stood next to Mrs Bold, placing his hand affectionately on her shoulder. Bobby, Betty and Miranda were almost asleep, their faces relaxed, smiles hovering on their lips.

'And Miss Paulina the otter, Craig the wild boar, Snappy the goose – all are happy now! Don't be sad. Be pleased, my dears. We Bolds have played a part in *all* this happiness. This should make you happy too. Be very happy to be a Bold!'

'Of course, another good way to be happy is to have a jolly good laugh,' added Mr Bold.

'Tell us a goodnight joke, Dad,' murmured Betty.

Mrs Bold gave a little tut.

'Very well,' said Mr Bold.

> What's the difference between a schoolteacher and a train?

> A teacher says, "Spit out your gum", and the train says, "Chew, chew, chew!"

The twins' smiles grew even **wider**, and then at last they fell into a deep happy sleep.

The End

MR BOLD'S JOKES

What does a cloud wear under its raincoat?
Thunderwear!

Where does a caterpillar buy his clothes?
A cater-logue!

What's a caterpillar's favourite weapon?
A cater-pault!

What is the definition of a caterpillar?
A worm in a fur coat!

What do you get if you cross a clock with a chicken?
A cluck!

What did the watch say to the clock?
'Hour you doing?'

What did the robber say to the clock?
'Hands up!'

Why can't dogs drive?
Because they can't find a barking space!

Why did the belt go to jail?
Because he held up a pair of trousers!

Knock, knock!
Who's there?
Tyrone.
Tyrone who?
Tyrone shoelaces!

Knock, knock!
Who's there?
Olive.
Olive who?
Olive next door!

Knock, knock!
Who's there?
Nana
Nana who?
Nana your business!

What kind of shoes do frogs wear?
Open-toad!

Why did Grandma put wheels on her rocking chair?
Because she wanted to rock and roll!

What animal do you look like when you get in the bath?
A little bear!

How do you know there's a monster in your bath?
You can't get the shower curtain closed!

What kind of table can you eat?
A vege-table!

Which birds steal soap from the bath?
Robber ducks!

Why didn't the nose want to go to school?
He was tired of getting picked on!

What did the pencil sharpener say to the pencil?
'Stop going round in circles and get to the point!'

What vegetables do librarians like?
Quiet peas!

What do elves learn in school?
The elf-abet!

What's red and flies and wobbles at the same time?
A jelly-copter!

How do you make a milkshake?
Give it a good scare!

What did the little tree say to the big tree?
'Leaf me alone!'

How do chimps make toast
Under the gorilla!

What do you get when dinosaurs crash their cars?
Tyrannosaurus wrecks!

Why was the broom late?
He overswept!

Where do chimps get their gossip from?
The ape vine!

What do you call a baby monkey?
A chimp off the old block!

What do you call an exploding monkey?
A bab-boom!

What's the best time to see gorillas in the wild?
Ape-ril!

What type of tree fits in your hand?
A palm tree!

What did the beaver say to the tree?
'It's been nice gnawing you!'

What's the difference between a schoolteacher and a train?

A teacher says, 'Spit out your gum', and the train says, 'Chew, chew, chew!'

How do you know when a yacht is happy?

When it hugs the shore!

What has four wheels and flies?

A rubbish truck!

Why was the woman fired from the car assembly line?

Because she was caught taking a brake!

Knock, knock!
Who's there?
Eileen.
Eileen who?
Eileen-ed over and fell in the water!